KEYS TO KINGDOM

Superior Saturday

KEYS TO THE KINGDOM

So far ...

#1 Mister Monday

#2 Grim Tuesday

#3 Drowned Wednesday

#4 Sir Thursday

#5 Lady Friday

#6 Superior Saturday

H NIX

KEYS TO THE
KINGDOM

BOOK SIX

Superior
Saturday

SCHOLASTIC INC.

New York Toronto London Auckland
Sydney Mexico City New Delhi Hong Kong

This book was originally published in hardcover by Scholastic Press in 2008.

ISBN 978-0-439-43659-5

12 11 10 9 8 7 6 5 4 3 2 1   10 11 12 13 14 15/0

Printed in the U.S.A.   40

First Scholastic paperback printing, February 2010

The display type was set in Dalliance and Albertus.
The text type was set in Sabon.
Book design by Steve Scott

To all the patient readers and publishing folk who have been waiting for me to finish this book. And, as always, to Anna, Thomas, and Edward, and all my family and friends.

Prologue

Saturday, self-styled Superior Sorcerer of the House, stood in her private viewing chamber at the very apex of her dominion, atop the tower that she had been building for almost ten thousand years. This clear crystal-walled room was always at the top, the builders lifting it higher and higher as new levels were slotted in below.

Saturday looked down through the rain-washed glass, at the multitude of fuzzy green spots of light below. It looked like the tower, thousands of feet high, had suffered a vast, vertical infestation of green glow-worms, but the spots of light actually came from the green-shaded lamps that sat on every desk in the Upper House, in exactly the same position, just as each desk was set exactly in the middle of an open cube of red wrought iron, with a grille floor and no ceiling.

These cubes — the basic building blocks of Saturday's tower — ran on vertical and horizontal rails, ascending, descending, or moving sideways according to the merits of the Denizens who worked at the desks.

Each cube was dragged into place by a series of chains that were driven by mighty steam engines, deep below the tower. The actual work of building the rails and fueling the engines was done by bronze automatons and a small number of luckless Denizens who had failed Saturday in some way. Even lower in status were the grease monkeys, Piper's children who oiled and maintained the miles and miles of dangerous, fast-moving machinery.

Superior Saturday looked down upon her domain, but the sight of her mighty tower and the tens of thousands of sorcerers within it did not quicken her pulse. Eventually, though she fought against the urge, she stopped looking down and started looking up.

At first she saw only cloud, but then came a glimmer of green light, a darker, more mysterious green than the glow of her lamps. The clouds parted slightly to show the emerald ceiling of the Upper House, which was also the floor of the Incomparable Gardens. Saturday grimaced, an ugly look on her otherwise extraordinarily beautiful face. For ten thousand years she had been building her tower in order to reach and invade the Incomparable Gardens. Yet no matter how high she built, the Gardens moved farther away, and Lord Sunday taunted her by making sure she was the only one to see it. If any of her Denizens looked up, the clouds would close again.

Saturday curled her lip and looked away, but her new view offered no solace. Far off, on the edge of the Upper House, there was a dark vertical shadow that stretched from the ground to the clouds. Close up, it too would shine green, for it was a vast tree, one of the four Drasil trees that supported the Incomparable Gardens above.

The Drasil trees were the reason Saturday could never build her tower high enough, because the trees grew faster than she could build, and lifted the Gardens as they grew.

She had tried to destroy or stunt the Drasils with sorcery, poison, and brute force, but none of her schemes had affected the trees in the slightest. She had sent Artful Loungers and Sorcerous Supernumeraries to climb the trunks and infiltrate the domain of Lord Sunday, but they had never made it farther than halfway up, defeated by the huge defensive insects that lived in tunnels within the bark of the great trees. Even flying was out of the question. High above the clouds, the Drasils' branches spread everywhere, and the trees' limbs were predatory, vicious, and very fast.

This had been the situation for millennia, with Saturday building, the Drasils growing, and Sunday remaining aloof and mighty above, secure in the Incomparable Gardens.

But all that had changed with a sneeze on the surface of a distant, dead star. The Architect's Will had finally been released and had selected a Rightful Heir. Now that Heir was gathering the Keys from the disloyal Trustees. Arthur, his name was — a mortal whose success and speed had surprised not only Saturday.

Not that Arthur's triumphs mattered too much to Saturday, given that she had been planning for the execution of the Will and the arrival of an Heir almost since the moment the Architect disappeared. She was not just a Trustee, with the power the Architect's Key gave her; she was also an enormously powerful and learned sorcerer in her own right. Apart from the Old One and the Architect, she was the most ancient entity in the Universe. Therein lay the canker in her heart. She was the first Denizen the Architect had made, and she felt she should have been supreme over all others, including the Architect's children (an experiment she had decried at the time). It was not Sunday who should dwell in the Incomparable Gardens, but Saturday. Everything she did was directed to remedying this injustice.

A muffled cough behind her recalled Saturday to present events. She turned, her cloak of starshine and moonshade billowing up around her shapely legs. Apart from the cloak, which was an ancient thing of sorcery, Saturday wore a robe of spun gold scattered with tiny sapphires, and high-heeled shoes that were made of steel and had vicious points. Her long electric-blue hair was loose on her shoulders and restrained at the brow by a gold circlet on which sorcerous words looped and writhed, spelled out in shifting diamonds.

"I beg your pardon, Majesty," said a tall, impeccably dressed Denizen. He knelt as she turned around, his swallow-tailed coat falling on his impossibly shiny boot heels.

"You are the candidate to be my new Dusk," said Saturday.

The Denizen bowed his head still lower, indicating agreement.

"The former Dusk was your brother? Turned out of the same mold?"

"Yes, Majesty, the elder of us by a moment."

"Good," said Saturday. "He served me well, and was at least partially successful in his last assignment, though he met his end. Has Noon acquainted you with all the matters at hand?"

"I believe so, Majesty," said the new Saturday's Dusk.

Saturday flicked a finger, and her Dusk stood up. Though he was easily seven feet tall, his mistress was at least a foot taller, even without her steel shoes. In any case, he kept his head bowed, not daring to look her in the eye.

"Tell me, then," she said. "Do all my enterprises conjoin for the final victory?"

"We believe so," said Dusk. "Though the House does not crumble as swiftly as was hoped at one time, it does fall, and our new offensive should accelerate matters. At present, our reports show that Nothing has impinged greatly into the Far Reaches and across large areas of the Border Sea and, though it is not related to our activities, there has been some considerable damage to the mountain defenses of the Great Maze. It is now almost certainly beyond the power of Dame Primus, as the Will calls itself, and its cat's-paw, Arthur, to prevent the destruction."

"Good," said Saturday. "What of the effect upon the trees?"

"As the Nothing spreads, the deeper roots of the Drasil are severed. This has already slowed their growth by some six percent. However, they still lift the Gardens faster than we can build. Projections indicate that when the entirety of the Far Reaches and the Lower House have been devoured by the Nothing, we will be able to build faster than the trees can grow, and can reach the target position in days. If more of the House falls, it will be a matter of hours."

"Excellent!" cried Saturday, a smile rippling across her shining, blue-painted lips. "I trust the Front Door remains closed, and the elevators secured? I want no interference from Primus or the Piper."

"The Front Door remains shut, though the Lieutenant

Keeper has petitioned the Court of Days for it to be reopened. So if Lord Sunday —"

"Sunday immures himself in the Gardens," Saturday interrupted. "He cares not for anything else. He will not interfere — at least not until it is too late for him to do anything."

"As you say, Majesty," said Dusk diplomatically. "All elevator entrances into the Upper House have been sealed and are guarded, but it is believed that renegade operators have opened some services in other parts of the House."

"Let them run about the ruins," said Saturday. "The sorceries against the Improbable Stair and the Fifth Key remain constant?"

"Four shifts of nine hundred sorcerers each maintain the wards. Twenty-eight hundred executive-level sorcerers wait at ready desks, should they need to counter any workings of the Keys held by the Pretender or a sorcerous attack from the Piper."

"The Piper!" Saturday spat. "If only I had managed to finish him centuries ago! At least he blames his brother. What is the latest news of the Piper? Have we gotten rid of his blasted rats?"

Dusk proceeded with caution. "We are not absolutely clear on what the Piper is doing. His forces have withdrawn from the Great Maze, presumably to the worldlet he made for his New Nithlings. But we have not yet located that worldlet, nor do we know if he masses his forces there against us or against Dame Primus."

"Our defenses will hold as well against the Piper as they will against the Pretender," Saturday stated confidently. "They cannot enter via elevator, Stair, Front Door, or by use of the Fifth Key. There is no other way."

Saturday's Dusk did not speak, but the faintest frown line appeared on his forehead, just for a moment, before he smoothed it away.

"And the Rats?" prompted Saturday.

"None have been spotted in five days. We have lost fourteen lower-level Clerks and some Piper's children to the Rat-catcher automatons, and there have been requests that they be recalled."

"No," said Saturday. "Keep them at it. I do not want those creatures sneaking about here."

"Speaking of Piper's children, we employ a large number of them as grease monkeys and chain-hands, but there was a report that some of Sir Thursday's Piper's children were turned against him by the Piper. We would not want our Piper's children to be similarly turned against us."

"Yes," said Saturday. "He has power over his creations, and they must answer to his pipe. It is not an eventuality that should arise, if he is kept out of the Upper House, and we need those children to maintain our building speed. However, we should be prepared. Tell Noon to detail a suitable number of Sorcerous Supernumeraries to shadow the Piper's children — and slay them, if I so command."

"Very good, Majesty," said Dusk. "There is one other matter. . . ."

"Yes?"

"The Pretender, this Arthur Penhaligon. We have just had a report that he has returned to the Secondary Realms, to Earth. Do we implement the contingency plan?"

Saturday smiled.

"Yes, at once. Do we know if he has a Key with him?"

"We do not know, Majesty, but circumstance suggests he has at least the Fifth Key."

"I wonder if that will protect him. It will be interesting to see. Tell Pravuil to act at once."

"Ahem . . ." Dusk coughed. "I regret to say that it is not yet Saturday on Earth, Majesty. It is some forty minutes short of Friday's midnight, and the House and that Secondary Realm are in close temporal step."

Saturday hesitated, weighing the situation. The Accord between the Trustees was effectively broken, but the treaty still existed, and there could be sorcerous implications if she or her agents acted outside their allotted span of power in the Secondary Realms.

"Then Pravuil must strike as the twelfth chime of midnight fades," she instructed. "In the first second of Saturday. No later. See to it at once."

"Yes, Majesty," replied the new Dusk. After an elegant bow, he retreated to the silver spiral stair that led down to the desk cube immediately beneath the viewing chamber.

As soon as he was gone, Superior Saturday's gaze was once again drawn to the sky, the parting clouds, and another infuriating but tantalizing glimpse of the underside of the Incomparable Gardens.

Chapter One

It was dark outside the small private hospital, the street-lights out and the houses across the road shut up tight. Only the faintest glowing lines around some windows indicated that there were probably people inside, and that the city still had power. There were other lights in the sky, but these were the navigation lights of helicopters, tiny pinprick red dots circling high above. Occasionally a searchlight flickered down from one of the helicopters, closely followed by the harsh clatter of machine-gun fire.

Inside the hospital, a flash of light suddenly lit up the empty swimming pool, accompanied by a thunderclap that rattled every window and drowned the distant sounds of the choppers and gunfire. As the light from the flash slowly faded, a slow, regular drumbeat echoed through the halls.

In the front office, a tired woman clad in a crumpled blue hospital uniform looked away from the videoscreen that was carrying the latest very bad news and jumped up to flick on the corridor lights. Then she grabbed her mop and bucket and ran. The thunderclap and drumming announced the arrival of Doctor Friday, and Doctor Friday always wanted the floors cleaned ahead of her, so she could see her reflection in the glossy surface of the freshly washed linoleum.

The cleaner ran through the wards, turning on lights as she passed. Just before the pool room, she glanced at her watch. It was 11:15 on Friday night. Doctor Friday had never come so late before, but her servants sometimes did. In any case, the cleaner was not allowed to leave until the day was completely done. Not that there was anywhere to go, with the new quarantine in force and helicopters shooting anyone who ventured out onto the streets. The news was now also full of talk of a "last-resort solution" to the "plague nexus" that existed in the city.

Outside the pool room, the cleaner stopped to take a deep breath. Then she bent her head, dipped her mop, and pushed it and the bucket through the doors, reaching up to flick the light switch without looking, as she had done so many times, on so many Fridays past. She had learned long ago not to look up, because then she might meet Friday's gaze, or be dazzled by her mirror.

But it wasn't Friday or her minions who were emerging from the dark portal in the empty swimming pool and climbing up the ramp.

The cleaner stared at their bare feet and the blue

hospital nightgowns. She dropped her mop, looked up, and screamed.

"They're coming back! But they never come back!"

The sleepers that she had seen enter the pool only that morning, led by Doctor Friday herself, were shambling their way up, arms outstretched in front of them in the classic pose of sleepwalkers seen so often in films and television.

But this time Doctor Friday wasn't there, and neither were any of her ridiculously tall and good-looking assistants.

Then the cleaner saw the girl, the one who had been awake that morning. She was shepherding the very first sleeper, a woman at the head of the line, steering her to the center of the ramp. The sleepers weren't as obedient as they had been going out, or as deeply asleep.

"Hi!" called the girl. "Remember me?"

The cleaner nodded dumbly.

"My name's Leaf. What's yours?"

"Vess," whispered the cleaner.

"Give us a hand, then, Vess! We've got to get everyone into bed, at least for tonight."

"What . . . what about Doctor Friday?"

"She's gone," said Leaf. "Defeated by Arthur!"

She gestured behind her, and the cleaner saw a handsome young boy of a similar age to Leaf. His skin was almost glowing with good health, his hair was shiny, and his teeth were very white. But that was not the most striking thing about him. He held a light in his hand, a brilliant star that the cleaner recognized as Friday's mirror.

"Sir!" said the cleaner, and she went down on one knee and bent her head. Leaf frowned and looked back at Arthur, and in that moment saw him anew.

"What?" asked Arthur. "Hey, keep them walking or we'll get a pileup back here."

"Sorry," said Leaf. She hastily pulled the leading sleeper — her own aunt Mango — out of the line and held on to her arm. "It's . . . well, I just realized you look . . . you don't look the same as you used to."

Arthur looked down at himself and then up again, his face showing puzzlement.

"You used to be a bit shorter than me," said Leaf. "You've grown at least three or four inches and gotten . . . um . . . better looking."

"Have I?" muttered Arthur. Only a few weeks ago he would have been delighted to hear he was getting taller. Now it sent an unpleasant shiver through him. He glanced at the crocodile ring on his finger, the one that indicated just how far his blood and bone had been contaminated by sorcery. But before he could gauge how much of the ring had turned from silver to gold, he forced himself to look away. He didn't want to confirm right then and there if his transformation into a Denizen had gone beyond the point of no return. In his heart, he knew the answer without even looking at the ring.

"Never mind that now," continued Arthur. "We'd better get everyone settled down. What's your name again? Vess, we'll need your help getting all these sleepers back into bed, please. There's about two thousand of them, and we've only got Martine and Harrison to help."

"Martine and Harrison?" yelped Vess. "I haven't seen them in . . . I thought they were dead!"

"Martine and Harrison have been . . . looking after sleepers at Lady Friday's retreat," Arthur reported. "Hey! Leaf, they're running into the door!"

Leaf gently spun her aunt around to face the wall and sprinted ahead to guide the leading sleepers through the door, pressing down the stopper to keep it open. Then she took a small silver cone from her belt and held it to her mouth. The cone was one of the tools Friday's servants used to direct the sleepers. It amplified and changed Leaf's speech, and Vess shivered as she caught the echo of Lady Friday's voice.

"Walk to an empty bed and stand next to it," ordered Leaf. "Walk to an empty bed and stand next to it."

The sleepers obeyed, though they tended to bunch at a bed and bump against one another before one firmly established himself or herself next to the bedhead. Only then would the others shamble off. Leaf ran back to her aunt, who was turning in circles trying to obey the command to find a bed.

Arthur stayed back at the pool, repeating Leaf's instruction to the sleepers as they came through. He didn't need a silver cone to be obeyed, probably because he held the Fifth Key, or because the sleepers responded to the power in his voice, feeling the authority of his position as the Rightful Heir of the Architect.

In outward appearance he looked just like a boy, but Arthur had wrested five Keys from five of the faithless Trustees. Now he ruled over the majority of the House, the epicenter of the Universe. In the process he felt he had grown much older, even if little time had actually passed. He also knew that he was becoming less human.

The sleepers kept coming through, emerging out of the dark floor of the pool that was in fact a passage to another Secondary Realm, the secret retreat of Lady Friday, where she had been stealing humans' memories, leaving them as mindless husks. The sleepers who were being returned had narrowly avoided that fate. They would wake in due course, knowing nothing of their ordeal.

Martine, one of Lady Friday's human staff, emerged and nodded at Arthur before starting up the ramp. She had an expression on her face that Arthur guessed was equal parts fear and excitement. Martine had been forced to stay and work in Friday's retreat for more than thirty years.

She would find the contemporary world a very strange place, Arthur thought. A world that was getting stranger by the day — not least because the appearance of Denizens and Nithlings from the House had a bad effect upon the Secondary Realms like Earth, disrupting the environment on many different levels, including the spontaneous generation of new and deadly viruses.

Arthur thought about that as he watched the sleepers march, occasionally intervening to keep them moving. His presence now with the Fifth Key would undoubtedly destabilize something on Earth, maybe even create something really bad like the Sleepy Plague. He would not be able to linger, and perhaps should not even stay long enough to go home and check up on his family. But he desperately wanted to see if his sister Michaeli and brother Eric were all right, and also to find some clue to where his mother, Emily, might be, or who might have taken her, if Sneezer was correct and she was no longer on Earth at all.

A ringing phone interrupted his thoughts. It got louder and louder, closer and closer. Arthur scowled. He didn't have a cell phone, but the old-fashioned ring tone was coming from the pocket of his paper suit. . . .

He sighed, put the Fifth Key in his pocket, and rummaged around to see what else was in there. When his fingers closed on a small, cold tube he knew hadn't been there before, he pulled it out and found a full-size, antique candlestick-style phone with a separate earpiece that could neither have fitted into his pocket in the first place or come out of it if it had. It was, in other words, a perfectly normal manifestation of a House telephone, behaving according to its own magical rules.

"Yes?" said Arthur.

"Stand by," said a voice that sounded much more like a human telephone operator than a Denizen. "Thru-connecting now, sir."

"Who's that?" asked someone else. A familiar, masculine voice — again not a Denizen.

"Erazmuz!?" asked Arthur in surprise. Erazmuz was his oldest brother, a major in the army. How could he be calling on a House telephone?

"Arthur? How come the screen's off? Never mind. Is Emily home?"

"Uh, no," said Arthur. "I'm not —"

"Eric? Michaeli?"

Erazmuz was talking really fast, not letting Arthur get a word in, so he couldn't tell him that he wasn't home, even if it was the number that Erazmuz had dialed.

"No, they're not   "

"That's . . ."

Erazmus's voice trailed away for a second, then he came back, talking faster than ever.

"Okay . . . you've got to grab any bottled water and food like cans or packaged stuff and an opener, get warm clothes, and head down to the cellar as soon as you can, but no more than ten minutes from now, ten minutes maximum, okay? Shut it up tight and stay down there. Do you know where Emily and the others are?"

"No! What's going on?"

"General Pravuil has just flown in, and he's ordered the launch of four micronukes at what's left of East Area Hospital at 12:01. If you get to the cellar, you should be okay, just don't come out till I get there. I'll be with the cleanup —"

"What!" exclaimed Arthur. "Nukes! I can't believe you — the army — is going to nuke part of the city! There must be thousands of people —"

"Arthur! I shouldn't even be talking to you! Don't waste time!"

There was a clear sound of desperation in Erazmuz's voice.

"We can't stop it, the general's got every clearance — the hospital's been declared a viral plague nexus under the Creighton Act. Get water and food and some blankets and get down to the cellar *now*!"

The line went dead. The phone started to fade in Arthur's hand, becoming insubstantial, its sharp edges turning foggy and cold.

"Hold on," ordered Arthur. He tightened his grip. "I want to make a call."

The telephone solidified again. There was a sound like a distant choir singing, followed by some indistinct shouting. Then a light, silvery voice said, "Oh, get off, do. This is our exchange — we don't care what Saturday says. Operator here."

"This is Lord Arthur. I need to speak to Doctor Scamandros urgently, please. I'm not sure where he is — probably the Lower House."

"Ooh, Lord Arthur. It's a bit tricky right now. I'll do my best. Please hold."

Arthur lowered the phone for a second and looked around. He couldn't see a clock, and he had no idea what time of day it was. Nor did he know how close this private hospital was to the big East Area Hospital — it could be next door for all he knew. Leaf, Martine, and Vess were in the other rooms, settling down sleepers, so there wasn't anyone to ask. Many more of the old folk continued to shamble past.

Arthur ran up the ramp, narrowly missing slowly swinging elbows and widely planted feet. He kept the earpiece to his head, but he couldn't hear anything now, not even the shouting in the background.

"Leaf! Leaf! What time is it?" he shouted in the general direction of the door. Then he raised the telephone and, hardly lowering his voice, insisted, "I *must* speak to Doctor Scamandros! Quickly, please!"

Chapter Two

Leaf came running back as Arthur ran forward, and the two nearly collided at the door. In recovering, they turned several sleepers around. It took a moment to get them sorted out, with Arthur still trying to hold the phone.

"What time is it?" Arthur asked again.

"Time? I wouldn't have a clue," puffed Leaf. "It's nighttime outside."

"Ask Vess, quickly. The army is going to nuke East Area Hospital at 12:01 Saturday morning!"

"What!?" shrieked Leaf.

"I can probably do something," said Arthur hastily. "I have to check with Doctor Scamandros. Find out how close to East Area we are!"

Leaf turned and ran. Arthur pressed his ear harder against the phone, thinking he heard something. But the only sound was the shuffle of the sleepers as they slowly passed by him. The telephone itself was silent.

"Come on, come on," whispered Arthur anxiously, half into the telephone, half out into the air. He had an idea about something he could do, but he needed to check with Scamandros about exactly how to do it and what could go wrong.

No answer came from the phone, but Leaf came running back.

"It's ten minutes to midnight on Friday night!" she shouted. "We're less than half a mile away from East Area. This even used to be part of the big hospital years ago!"

She skidded to a halt next to Arthur and gulped down several panicked breaths.

"What are you going to do? We've only got ten minutes!"

"Hello!" Arthur shouted into the telephone. "Hello! I have to speak to Doctor Scamandros *now*!"

There was no answer. Arthur gripped the phone even tighter, willing it to connect, but that didn't help.

"Probably nine minutes, now," said Leaf. "You've got to do something, Arthur!"

Arthur glanced at the crocodile ring very quickly. Leaf saw him look.

"Maybe Scamandros is wrong about the sorcerous contamination," she said. "Or the ring doesn't measure very well."

"It's okay, Leaf," said Arthur slowly. "I've been thinking about all that anyway. You know why the Will chose me to be the Rightful Heir, how it tricked Mister Monday? I was going to die . . . but getting the First Key saved me —"

"Sure, I remember," said Leaf hastily. "Now we're all going to die unless you do something!"

"I am going to do something," said Arthur. "That's what I'm explaining to you. I've worked out that I was going to die anyway, so everything I've done — everything I do from now on — is a kind of bonus anyway. Even if I turn into a Denizen, I'll still be alive and at least I can help other people —"

"Arthur, I understand!" Leaf interrupted. "Just do something, please! We can talk afterwards!"

"Okay," said Arthur. He dropped the telephone. As it fell, it turned into a shower of tiny motes of light that faded and were gone before they hit the floor.

Arthur took a deep breath, and for a moment marveled at just how deeply he could breathe now, his asthma gone with his old human self, all earthly frailties being left behind in his transition to a new, immortal form. Then he took the mirror that was the Fifth Key out of his pocket and held it up in front of his face. An intense light shone around it in a fierce corona, but Arthur looked directly at the mirror without difficulty, seeing only the reflection of his own changing face, his more regular nose, his whiter teeth, and his silkier hair.

Leaf shielded her eyes with her arm, and even the sleep-walkers turned their heads away and screwed their eyes shut tighter as they kept shuffling forward.

I really hope this works, thought Arthur. *It has to work. Only I wish I could have checked with Dr. Scamandros, because I don't really know what . . .*

Arthur grimaced, banished his fearful inner voice, and focused on what he wanted the Fifth Key to do. Because it seemed easier and somehow made it sound more like it would happen, he spoke aloud to the Key.

"Fifth Key of the Architect! I, Arthur Penhaligon, Rightful Heir of the Architect, um . . . I desire you to shield this city inside a bubble that keeps it separate from Earth, a bubble that will protect the city and keep everyone in it safe from all harm, and . . . well . . . that's it . . . thanks."

The mirror flashed and this time Arthur did have to blink. When he opened his eyes, he felt momentarily unsteady on his feet and had to raise his arms like a tight-rope-walker to regain his balance. In that instant, he saw that everyone else had stopped moving. Leaf and the line of sleepers were still, as if they had been snap-frozen. Many of the sleepers had one foot slightly off the ground, a position that no one could possibly keep up in normal circumstances.

It was also newly quiet. Arthur couldn't hear the helicopters or gunfire or any other noise. It was like being in a waxwork museum after closing time, surrounded by posed statues.

Arthur slipped the mirror into his pocket and ran his fingers through his hair — which had gotten considerably longer than he cared for, though it somehow stayed out of his face.

"Leaf?" he said tentatively, walking over to tap his friend lightly on the shoulder. "Leaf? Are you okay?"

Leaf didn't move. Arthur looked at her face. Her eyes were open but her pupils didn't move when he waved his finger back and forth. He couldn't even tell if she was breathing.

Arthur felt a sudden panic rise in him.

I've killed them, he thought. *I was trying to save them, but I killed them. . . .*

He touched Leaf on the shoulder again, and though a faint nimbus of red light sprang up around his fingers, she still didn't move or react in any way.

Arthur stepped back and looked around. There was a faint red glow around each of the sleepers too, and when he walked over and touched them, this light also grew momentarily brighter. Arthur didn't know what the glow meant, but he found it slightly comforting, as it suggested some sorcerous effect was active and he hadn't just killed everyone.

But I don't even know if I have protected us from the nukes, Arthur thought. *What time is it?*

He turned and ran down the hall, through the next two wards, and out into the lobby. From there it took him a minute to find the office and a clock. It had stopped at exactly 11:57, the second hand quivering on the twelve. The clock also had a faint red sheen, and there were ghostly scarlet shadows behind the second and hour hands.

Arthur ran outside. The front doors slammed shut behind him with a sound all too like the trump of doom. He slid to a halt just before he fell down the wheelchair ramp, because everywhere he looked was tinted red. It was like looking at the world through red sunglasses on an overcast day, because the night sky had been replaced by a solid red that was buzzing and shifting and hard to look at, like a traffic light viewed far too close.

"I guess I've done *something*," Arthur said to himself. "I just don't know exactly what. . . ."

He walked a little farther, out into the parking lot. Something caught his eye, up in the sky, a small silhouette. He peered at it for a few seconds before he worked out that it was a helicopter gunship. But it wasn't moving. It was like a model stuck on a piece of wire in a diorama, just hanging there in the red-washed sky.

Stuck in a moment of time.

That's why everyone is frozen in place, Arthur thought. *I've stopped time . . . that's how the Key is keeping everyone in the city safe. . . .*

If time was only frozen or slowed inside a bubble around the city, it could start again, or be started again by some other power. Which meant that the nuclear strike on East Area Hospital would still happen. He hadn't saved the city from the attack. He'd just postponed it. . . .

"If it isn't one thing, it's another," whispered Arthur. He looked along the empty street, all strange and red-hued, and wondered if he should run over to his home and see if his family was all right. Maybe he could carry them down into the cellar . . . but if he did that, he might be wasting time better spent in learning how to protect everyone else. He couldn't carry everyone in danger to safety.

He'd gained a breathing space for the city, and he could extend it by going back to the House. If he left now, he should be able to return to almost exactly the same time, even if he spent days or even weeks in the House.

Should is not the same as definitely, thought Arthur grimly. *I wish I understood the time relativities better. I wish I knew more about how to use the Keys. I wish I'd never, ever got involved in all —*

Arthur stopped himself.

"If I wasn't involved, I'd be dead," he said aloud. "I just have to get on with it."

Getting on with it, Arthur thought, included facing up to things. He held his hand up close to his face and looked at the crocodile ring. Even in the weird red light, he could see it clearly. The diamond eyes of the crocodile looked baleful, as dark as dried black blood rather than their usual pink. The ten marked sections of its body, each inscribed with a Roman numeral, recorded the degree of sorcerous contamination in his blood and bone. If more than six sections had turned from silver to gold, Arthur would be permanently tainted with sorcery and irretrievably destined to become a Denizen.

Arthur slowly turned the ring around, to see how far the gold transformation had progressed, counting in his head. One, two, three, four, five . . . he knew it had gone that far already. He turned the ring again, and saw the gold had completely filled the fifth segment, and had flooded over, almost completely across the sixth segment.

I am . . . I am going to be a Denizen.

Arthur took a deep, shuddering breath and looked

again, but there was no change in the ring. It was six parts gold. He was sixty percent immortal.

"No turning back now," said Arthur to the red world around him. "Time to get back to work."

He looked away from the ring and lowered his hand. Bending his head for a moment, he drew out the Fifth Key from his pocket and raised it high. According to Dame Primus, the mirror of Lady Friday could take him to anywhere he had previously seen within the House, if there was a reflective surface there.

Arthur pictured the throne room in the Lower House, the big audience chamber where he had met with Dame Primus and everyone before he was drafted into the Army of the Architect. It was the place he could most easily visualize in Monday's Dayroom, because it didn't have much detail and was so over the top in decoration — including floors of reflective marble.

"Fifth Key, take me to the throne room in Monday's Dayroom."

The Fifth Key shivered in Arthur's hand and a beam of white light sprang from it, banishing the red. The light formed a perfect, upright rectangle, exactly like a door.

Arthur walked into the rectangle of light and disappeared from his own city, from his Earth, perhaps never to return.

Chapter Three

The throne room was empty. Otherwise it looked the same as it had when Arthur had last been there: like one enormous, ritzy, poorly conceived hotel bathroom. It was about as large as a big city theater, and the walls, floor, and ceiling were all lined with gold-veined white marble that was polished to a highly reflective sheen.

The vast, red-iron round table was still in the middle of the chamber, with the hundred tall-backed white chairs around it. On the other side, Arthur's own high throne of gilded iron sat next to the rainbow chair of Dame Primus.

"Hello!" Arthur called out. "Anyone here?"

His voice filled the empty space, and the echoes were the only answer. Arthur sighed and strode over to the door, his footsteps setting up another echo behind him, so it sounded like he was being followed by many small, close companions.

The corridor outside was still crowded with thousands of bundles of paper, each tied with a red ribbon and stacked like bricks. Unlike last time, there were no Commissionaire

Sergeants standing at attention in the gaps between the piles of paperwork.

"Hello!" Arthur shouted again. He ran down the corridor, pausing several times to see if there were doors leading out. Eventually he came to the end of the corridor, where he found a door propped half open and partially covered in bundles of paper. He could only see it because one of the piles had collapsed.

There were still no Denizens. Arthur rushed through the half-open door and along another empty corridor, pushing doors open as he passed them without encountering anyone else.

"Hello! Anyone here?" he shouted every few yards, but no answer came.

Finally he came to a pair of tall, arched doors of dark oak. They were barred, but he easily lifted the bar — not even pausing to marvel that he had grown so strong that he could move a piece of timber that must weigh several hundred pounds. Once the bar was up, the door was easily pushed open.

This particular door led outside. Arthur had expected to see the lake and the rim of the crater that surrounded the Dayroom, and the ceiling of the Lower House above. Instead he saw a vast, arching wave of Nothing that rose way above him, a wave that had already eaten up everything but the small villa behind him. He felt like he was on a small hilltop, the last piece of dry land ahead of a tsunami — but the wave was coming, climbing high, and it would soon crash down to destroy even this last refuge.

Arthur turned to run, his heart suddenly hammering in fear, his mouth dry as dust. But after that first panicked step, he stopped and turned back. The wave of Nothing was coming down, and he didn't have time to run. He doubted the Fifth Key could protect him from such a vast influx of Nothing. At least not unless he actively directed its power.

I have to do something, thought Arthur, and he acted with the speed of that thought.

Even as the wave of Nothing crashed down upon him, he raised the mirror and held it high, pushing it toward the dark, falling sky.

"Stop!" he shouted, his voice raw with power, every part of his mind focused on stopping the tsunami of Nothing. "Stop! By the Keys I hold, I order the Nothing to stop! House, you must hold against the Void!"

Blinding light shone from the mirror, hot white beams that set the air on fire as they shot out and up, striking the onrush of Nothing, splashing across the face of the darkness, small marks of brilliance upon the void.

Arthur felt a terrible pain blossom in his heart. The

pain spread, racing down his arms and legs. Awful crack-
ing sounds came from his joints, and he had to screw his
eyes shut and scream as his teeth rearranged themselves
into a more perfect order in his jaw. Then his jaw itself
moved and he felt the plates of bone in his skull shift and
change.

But still he kept holding the mirror up above his head,
even as he fell to his knees. He used the pain, channeling it
to fuel his concentration, directing his will against the rush
of Nothing.

Finally, it was too much. Arthur could neither bear the
pain nor continue the effort. He fell forward on his face,
his screams becoming dull sobs. His strength used up, he
dropped the Fifth Key on the narrow band of grass that
was all that remained of the lawns that had once surrounded the Dayroom villa.

He lay there, partially stunned, awaiting annihilation,
knowing that he had failed and that when he died, the rest
of the Universe would follow. All he loved would be
destroyed, back on Earth, in the House, and in the worlds
beyond.

A minute passed, and then another, and the annihilation didn't happen. As the pain in his bones ebbed, Arthur
groaned and rolled over. He would face the Nothing, rather

than be snuffed out by it while he lay defeated upon the grass.

The first thing he saw was not incipient destruction but a delicate tracery of glowing golden lines, like a web or a mesh net of light thrown against the sky. It was holding back the great mass of threatening darkness, but Arthur could feel the pressure of the Nothing, could feel the infinite Void pushing against his restraints. He knew that it would soon overcome his net of light and once again advance.

Arthur picked up the mirror and staggered to his feet. The ground felt farther away than normal, and he lost his balance for a moment, swaying on the spot. The sensation passed as he shook his head, and he ran back to the open doors. There was a telephone in the library, he knew, and he needed to call and find out where in the House was safe, instead of going somewhere that might have already succumbed to Nothing. He didn't want to think about what would happen if he used the Fifth Key to take him straight into the Void, though it probably would have the advantage of being quick. . . .

Or maybe the Key would protect me for a little while, Arthur thought with sudden nausea. *Long enough to feel the Nothing dissolve my flesh . . .*

He hurried along the main corridor until he saw a door he recognized. Darting through it, he leaped up the steps four at a time, bouncing off the walls as he tried to take the turns in the staircase too fast.

At the top, he sprinted down another long corridor, this one also narrowed by piles of records, many of them written on papyrus or cured hides instead of paper. Pausing to shift a six-foot-high stone tablet that had fallen and blocked the way, Arthur didn't bother with the handle of the door at the end but kicked it open and stumbled into the library beyond.

The room was empty, and not just of Denizens. The books were gone from the shelves, as were the comfortable leather armchairs and the carpet. Even the scarlet bell rope that Sneezer had pulled to reveal the heptagonal room that housed the grandfather clocks of the Seven Dials was missing, though the room was presumably still there, behind the bookcase.

The telephone that had stood on a side table was also missing.

Arthur's shoulders slumped. He could feel the pressure outside, like a sinus pain across his forehead. He knew it was the weight of Nothing striving to break the bonds he had placed upon it. The weight was there in his mind, making him weary, almost too weary to think straight.

"Telephone," mumbled Arthur, holding out his right hand, while he cradled the Fifth Key in his left. "I need a telephone, please. Now."

Without further ado, a telephone appeared in his hand. Arthur set it down on the floor and sat next to it, lifting the earpiece and bending to speak into the receiver. He could hear crackling and buzzing, and in the distance someone was singing something that sounded rather like "Raindrops keep falling on my head," but the words were "Line-drops are lining up tonight."

"Hello, it's Lord Arthur. I need to speak to Dame Primus. Or Sneezer. Or anyone, really."

The singing abruptly stopped, replaced by a thin, soft voice that sounded like paper rustling.

"Ah, where are you calling from? This line doesn't appear to be technically, um, attached to anything."

"The Lower House," said Arthur. "Please, I think I'm about to be engulfed by Nothing and I need to work out where to go."

"Easier said than done," replied the voice. "Have you ever tried connecting a non-existent line to a switchboard that isn't there anymore?"

"No," said Arthur. Somewhere outside he heard a twanging sound, like a guitar string snapping. He felt it too, a sudden lurch in his stomach. His net, his defense against the Void, was breaking. "Please hurry!"

"I can get Doctor Scamandros — will he do?" asked the operator. "You wanted him before, it says here —"

"Where is he?" gabbled Arthur.

"The Deep Coal Cellar, which is kind of odd," said the operator. "Since nothing else in the Lower House is still connected . . . but metaphysical diversion was never my strong suit. Shall I put you through? Hello . . . hello . . . are you there, Lord Arthur?"

Arthur dropped the phone and stood up, not waiting to hear more. He raised the mirror that was the Fifth Key and concentrated upon it, desiring to see out of the reflective surface of a pool of water in the Deep Coal Cellar — if there was such a pool of water, and a source of light.

He was distracted for an instant by the sight of his own face, which was both familiar and strange. Familiar, because it was in essence much the same as it had been at any other time he'd looked in a mirror, and strange because there were numerous small changes. His cheekbones had become a little more pronounced, the shape of his head was a bit different, his ears had gotten smaller. . . .

"The Deep Coal Cellar!" snapped Arthur at the mirror,

both to distract himself and get on with his urgent task: finding somewhere to escape to before Nothing destroyed Monday's Dayroom.

His image wavered and was replaced by a badly lit scene that showed an oil lamp perched on a very thick, leather-bound book the size of several house bricks, which was set atop a somewhat collapsed pyramid made from small pieces of coal. The lamplight was dim, but Arthur could perceive someone on the far side of the pyramid who was raising a fishing pole over his head, ready to cast. Arthur saw only the caster's hands and two mustard-yellow cuffs, which he immediately recognized.

"Fifth Key," Arthur commanded, "take me to the Deep Coal Cellar, next to Doctor Scamandros."

As before, a door of pure white light appeared. As Arthur stepped through it, he felt his defensive net tear asunder behind him and the onrush of the great wave of Nothing.

A scant few seconds after his escape, the last surviving remnants of the Lower House ceased to exist.

Chapter Four

Arthur appeared next to a pyramid of coal, stepping out of the air and frightening the life out of a short, bald Denizen in a yellow greatcoat, who dropped his fishing pole, jumped back, and pulled a smoking bronze ball that looked like a medieval hand grenade out of one of his voluminous pockets.

"Doctor Scamandros!" exclaimed Arthur. "It's me!"

"Lord Arthur!"

The tattooed trumpets on Dr. Scamandros's forehead blew apart into clouds of confetti. He tried to pinch out the fuse on the smoking ball, but a flame ran around his fingers and continued on its way. Even more smoke boiled out of the infernal device.

"Scamand —" Arthur started to say, but Scamandros interrupted him, lobbing the ball behind a particularly large pyramid of coal some thirty feet distant.

"One moment, Lord Arthur."

There was a deafening crack and a fierce rush of air, closely followed by a great gout of smoke and coal dust that spiraled up into the air. Moments later, a hail of coal came down, some fist-sized pieces striking the ground uncomfortably close to the sorcerer and the boy.

"I do beg your pardon, Lord Arthur," said Dr. Scamandros. Puffing slightly, he went down on one knee, clouds of disturbed coal dust billowing up almost as high as his shoulders. "Welcome."

"Please, do get up," said Arthur. He leaned forward and helped the Denizen rise. Dr. Scamandros was amazingly heavy, or possibly all the things he had in the pockets of his yellow greatcoat were amazingly heavy.

"What's going on?" Arthur asked. "I came back to Monday's Dayroom, but there was this . . . this huge wave of Nothing! I only just managed to hold it off long enough to escape."

"I fear that I lack exact knowledge of what has occurred," replied Scamandros. The tattoos on his face became a tribe of confused donkeys that ran in a circle from his chin to the bridge of his nose and back again, and kicked their heels at one another. "I have been here since we parted company at Lady Friday's retreat, a matter of some days. Dame Primus wished me to investigate some unusual phenomena, including the sudden growth of flowers and a powerful aroma of rose oil. It has been quite a restful interlude in some ways, though I have to say that attar of roses is no longer . . ."

The Denizen noticed Arthur's frown and got back to the question.

"Ahem, that is to say, just under an hour ago, I felt a tremor underfoot, followed a moment later by a sudden onslaught of Nothing that annihilated at least a third of the Cellar before its advance slowed. Fortunately it was not the third I happened to be located in at the time. I immediately attempted to telephone Dame Primus at the Citadel, but found all lines severed. Similarly, I was unable to summon an elevator. The few short experiments I have conducted suggest the following."

He held out three blackened fingers, closing them into his fist one by one.

"Item One. The defenses against the Void in the Far Reaches must have suddenly collapsed, allowing a huge surge of Nothing to smash through.

"Item Two. If you encountered a wave of Nothing as high as Monday's Dayroom, then it is likely that the entire Far Reaches and all of the Lower House have been destroyed. But there is a brighter note, which I shall label as Item Three.

"Item Three. If you got an operator on the line, the bulwark between the Lower and Middle House must have held. Or be holding, though everything below it has been lost."

"Everything? But here . . . where we are right now," asked Arthur. "This is part of the Lower House, how come it's not . . . uh . . . gone?"

"The Old One's prison is very strong," said Scamandros. He pointed to his left. Arthur looked and saw in the distance the faint sheen of blue light that he knew came from the clock face where the Old One was chained. "The Architect had to make it particularly resistant, to keep the Old One in check. Being of such adamant stuff, it has held against the initial inrush of Nothing. But now it is but a small islet, lost in the Void. We are entirely surrounded, and totally cut off from the rest of the House. It is very interesting, but I have to confess I'm relieved you're here, Lord Arthur. Without you, I fear that —"

Scamandros paused. The tattooed donkeys hung their heads and slowly became tumbledown stone cairns, memorial markers for the fallen.

"I fear that I would find the current situation, interesting as it is, likely to be fatal in a relatively short space of time, given that Nothing is eating this small refuge at a rate of approximately a yard an hour."

"What? You were just saying this area is adamant and strong and all that!" protested Arthur. He peered into the darkness, but he couldn't tell whether he was looking at advancing Nothing or just couldn't see very far because the only immediate light came from the feeble lantern on the coal pile.

"Oh, the area *immediately* adjacent to the clock is doubtless proof against the Void," said Scamandros. "But before your arrival I was weighing up the relative ... er ... benefits of being throttled by the Old One as opposed to being dissolved by Nothing."

"The Old One wouldn't throttle you ... oh ... I guess he might," said Arthur. "He does hate Denizens. ..." Arthur stopped talking and looked over at the blue glow, thoughts of his very first encounter with the Old One going through his mind. He could well remember the feel of the prison chain around his neck. "I hope he'll still talk to me. Since I'm here, I want to ask him some questions."

Dr. Scamandros peered owlishly at Arthur, with his half-moon spectacles glinting on his forehead, helping him focus his invisible third and fourth eyes.

"It is true that the Old One has a fondness for mortals. But I think you are no longer mortal. What does my ... your ring indicate?"

Arthur looked. The gold had washed well into the seventh segment.

"About seventy-five percent contaminated," he said quietly. "I hope the Old One can recognize the quarter part of humanity inside me."

"Perhaps it would be best to simply depart," said Scamandros nervously. "Though I should say that the ring has a margin —"

"I do need to at least try to get some answers from him," said Arthur distractedly. "If I keep my distance it should be okay. Then we'd better get up to the Citadel and find out what's happening from Dame Primus. Oh, and I need to ask you about something I've done back on Earth. . . ."

Quickly Arthur described what he'd done with the Key, and the strangely red-lit environment of what appeared to be a town frozen in time.

"I cannot be entirely sure, Lord Arthur, without proper investigation," said Scamandros. "But as you suspected, you may have separated your entire world from the general procession of time in the Secondary Realms, or have temporally dislocated just a portion of it, around your town. In either case, the cessation will slowly erode. In due course the march of time will resume its normal beat, and everything that was to happen will occur unless you return and prevent it before the erosion of the cessation, which you should be able to do given the elasticity of time between the House and the Secondary Realms. I'm sure Sneezer could tell you more, using the Seven Dials."

"But the Seven Dials must have been destroyed," said Arthur. "With Monday's Dayroom." He stopped and slapped the side of his head. "And all the records stored in the Lower House. They must have been destroyed too! Doesn't that mean that whatever those records were about in the Secondary Realms will also be destroyed? My record was there!"

Scamandros shook his head.

"The Seven Dials will have moved to safety of its own accord, hopefully to some part of the House we control. As for the records, only dead observations are held in the Lower House. Admittedly their destruction will create holes in the past, but that is of no great concern. Monday must have been given your record temporarily, I presume by the Will, but it would normally have been held in the Upper House, as an active record."

"Sneezer gave it to me after I defeated Monday, but I left it behind," said Arthur. "So Dame Primus has probably got it."

"Unless it has returned to the Upper House. Such documents cannot be long held out of their proper place."

"But then Saturday can change my record and that would change me!" exclaimed Arthur. "She could destroy it . . . me . . . both!"

Scamandros shook his head again. A tattoo of a red-capped judge with a beaked nose appeared on his left cheek and also shook his head.

"No — even if Saturday knows where it is, she could not change or destroy it. Not once you had even a single Key."

"I feel like my head is going to explode." Arthur massaged his temples with his knuckles and sighed. "There's just too much . . . What are you doing?"

Scamandros paused in the act of removing a very large hand drill from inside his coat and a shining ten-inch-long drill bit from an external pocket.

"If I bore a hole in your skull just here," said Scamandros, tapping the side of his forehead, "it will relieve the pressure. I expect it is a side effect of your transformation into a higher Denizen —"

"I didn't mean my head was *actually* going to explode," said Arthur. "So you can put that drill away. I meant that I have too much to do, too much information to deal with. Too many problems!"

"Perhaps I can assist in some other fashion?" asked Scamandros as he stowed his tools away.

"No," sighed Arthur. "Wait here. I'm going to talk to the Old One."

"Um, Lord Arthur, I trust that I can move a little in that direction?" Scamandros pointed at a pile of coal a few yards away and added, "As I observe that the front half of yonder pyramid has ceased to exist . . ."

"Of course you can move!" snapped Arthur. He felt a peculiar rage rising in him, something he'd never felt before, an irritation at having to deal with lesser Denizens and inferior beings. For a moment he even felt like striking Scamandros, or forcing the Denizen to prostrate himself and beg forgiveness.

Then the feeling was past, replaced by a deep sense of mortification and shame. Arthur liked Scamandros and he did not like the way he had just felt toward the sorcerer, the proud anger that had fizzed up inside him, like a shaken bottle of soda ready to explode. He stopped and took a deep breath and reminded himself that he was just a boy who had a very tough job to do, and that he would need all the help he could get, from willing friends, not fearful servants.

I'm not going to become like one of the Trustees, thought Arthur firmly. At the back of his head, another little thought lay under that. *Or like Dame Primus . . .*

"Sorry, I'm sorry, Doctor Scamandros. I didn't mean to shout. I just . . . I'm a bit . . . um . . . anyway, do whatever you need to do to keep away from the Nothing. We'll get out of here soon."

Dr. Scamandros bowed low as Arthur walked away, and another baseball-sized grenade fell out of an inner pocket and immediately began to smoke. The Denizen tut-tutted, pinched the burning fuse out, and slipped it up his sleeve, which did not look like a secure place for it to go. However, it did not immediately fall out.

Arthur walked on, weaving between the pyramids of coal and splashing through the puddles of dirty coal-dust-tainted water. He remembered that he had been very cold when he'd last visited the Deep Coal Cellar, but it felt quite pleasant now to him, almost warm. Perhaps a side effect of the Nothing that now surrounded the place, he thought.

There were other changes too. As he drew closer to the blue illumination spread by the clock, Arthur noticed that many of the pyramids now sprouted flowers. Climbing roses twined up through the coal, and between the puddles, there were clumps of bluebells.

The bluebells spread as the ground climbed a little higher and got drier, the flowers now growing out of stone slates rather than a bed of coal dust, which was equally impossible but did not bother Arthur. He was fairly used to the House. Flowers growing out of coal and stone were far from the strangest things he had seen.

At the last pyramid, he stopped, as he had done all that time ago, when he had first cautiously approached the Old One's prison. The shimmering blue light was less annoying than it had been then, and he could see more clearly this time, even without calling on the Fifth Key to shed some kinder illumination.

Arthur saw a markedly different landscape from what it had been. Between him and the clock-prison was a solid carpet of bluebells, interspersed with clumps of tall yellow-green stalks that burst out at the top in profuse pale white flowers that were shaped a little like very elongated daffodils, but at the same time looked too alien to have come from the earth he knew.

The raised circular platform of stone, the clock face, was significantly smaller, as if it had been shrunk. It had been at least sixty feet in diameter, the length of the driveway at Arthur's own home. Now it was half that, and the Roman numerals that had stood upright around the rim were smaller and tarnished, much of their blue glow gone. Some of them were bent over at forty-five degrees or more, and the numbers and most of the rim were wreathed in climbing red and pink roses.

The metal hands had shrunk with the clock face, to

remain in proportion. Long, shining blue-steel chains still ran from the ends of the hands back through the central pivot, fastened at the other end to the manacles locked on the wrists of the Old One.

The Old One himself was not as Arthur had last seen him. He still looked like a giant barbarian hero, eight feet tall and heavily muscled, but his formerly old, almost-translucent skin was now sun-dark and supple. His once-stubbled head now sported a fine crop of clean white hair that was tied back behind his neck. He no longer wore just a loincloth, but had on a sleeveless leather jerkin and a pair of scarlet leggings that came down to just below his knees.

Where he once looked like a fallen, fading ancient of eighty or ninety, the Old One now looked like a super-fit sixty-year-old hero who could easily take on and defeat any number of lesser, younger foes.

The giant was sitting on the rim of the clock between the numbers three and four, slowly plucking the petals from a rose. He was half-turned away from Arthur, so the boy couldn't see the Old One's eyes — or, if it was soon after they had been torn from their sockets by the puppets within the clock, the empty, oozing sockets.

Thinking that was something he definitely did not want to see, Arthur craned his neck to check the position of the clock hands. The hour hand was at nine, and the minute hand at five, which relieved him on three counts. The Old One's eyes would have had plenty of time to grow back and his chains would be fairly tight, keeping him close to the clock. Perhaps most important, it also meant the torturer puppets would not be emerging for several hours.

Arthur stepped out and crossed the field of bluebells. Chains rattled as he approached, and the Old One stood to watch him. Arthur stopped thirty or forty feet from the clock. While the face had shrunk, he couldn't be sure the chains had as well, so he erred on the side of caution.

"Greetings, Old One!" he called.

"Greetings, boy," rumbled the Old One. "Or perhaps I can call you boy no longer. Arthur is your name, is it not?"

"Yes."

"Come sit with me. We will drink wine and talk."

"Do you promise you won't hurt me?" asked Arthur.

"You will be safe from all harm for the space of a quarter hour, as measured by this clock," replied the Old One. "You are mortal enough that I would not slay you like a wandering cockroach — or a Denizen of the House."

"Thanks," said Arthur. "I think."

He approached cautiously, but the Old One sat down again and, doubling over his chain, swept a space next to him clear of the thorny roses, to make a seat for Arthur.

Arthur perched gingerly next to him.

"Wine," said the Old One, holding out his hand.

A small stoneware jug flew up out of the ground without parting the bluebells. He caught it and tipped it up above his mouth, pouring out a long draught of resin-scented wine. Arthur could smell it very strongly and once again, it made him feel slightly ill.

"You called the wine with a poem last time," Arthur said hesitantly. He was thinking of the questions he wanted to ask, and wasn't sure how to start.

"It is the power of my will that shapes Nothing," replied the Old One. "It is true that many lesser beings need to sharpen their thoughts with speech or song when they deal with Nothing. I do not *need* to do so, though on occasion it may amuse me to essay some rhyme or poesy."

"I wanted to ask you some questions," said Arthur. "And to tell you something."

"Ask away," said the Old One. "I shall answer if I choose. As for the telling, if I do not like what I hear, it shall not make me stray from my promise. Whatever your speech, you may still have safe passage hence. If you do not overstay your allotted time."

He wiped his mouth with the back of his hand and proffered the jug. Arthur quickly shook his head, so the ancient drank again.

"You probably know more than anyone about the Architect," said Arthur. "So I wanted to ask you what happened to her? And what is the Will exactly, and what is it . . . she . . . going to do? I mean, I'm supposed to be the Rightful Heir and all, and I thought that meant that I was going to end up in charge of everything, whether I wanted to or not. Only now I'm not so sure."

"I knew the Architect long ago," said the Old One slowly. He drank a series of smaller mouthfuls before speaking again. "Yet not so well as I thought, or I would not have suffered here so long. I do not know what happened to her, save that it must have been at least in part of her own choosing. As for the Will, it is an expression of her power, set up to achieve some end. If you are the Rightful Heir, I would suggest the question you need ask is this: What exactly are you to inherit, and from whom?"

Arthur frowned.

"I don't want to be the Heir. I just want to get my old life back and make sure everyone is safe," he said. "But I can't get everything sorted out without using the Keys, and that's turning me into a Denizen. Scamandros made me a ring that says I'm six . . . more than six parts in ten . . . sorcerously contaminated, and it's irreversible. So I *will* become a Denizen, right?"

"Your body is assuming an immortal form — that is evident," said the Old One. "But not everything of immortal flesh is a Denizen. Remember, the Architect did not make the mortals of Earth. She made the stuff of life and sowed it across all creation. You mortals arose from the possibility she made and, though she always liked to think so, are consequently not of her direct design. There is more to you, and all mortals, than the simple flesh you inhabit."

"But can I become a normal boy again?"

"I do not know." The Old One drained the last of the wine from the jug, then threw it far past the light of the clock. The sound of its shattering came faint and distant from the darkness, reassurance that there was still solid ground out there — at least for a little while longer. "In general, one cannot go back. But in going forward, you may achieve some of what you desired of the past. If you can survive, anything may happen." The Old One plucked another rose, careless of its thorns, and held it beneath his nose. "Perhaps you will even be given flowers. The clock ticks, Arthur. Your time is almost sped."

"I have so many questions," said Arthur. "Can you give me another ten —"

The Old One put down his rose and looked at the boy with his fierce blue eyes, a gaze that would make the most superior Denizen quail and tremble.

"Never mind." Arthur gulped. "I just wanted to tell you that if I do end up in charge of everything, I'll do my best to set you free. It isn't right that the puppets should torture you."

The Old One blinked and took up the rose again.

"I honor you for that. But look — the puppets are no more. As the House has weakened, I have grown stronger. An hour ago, the clock shivered, and I felt Nothing draw close. The puppets felt it too, and as is their duty, came forth before their time, to prevent a rescue or an attempted escape. I fought with them, broke them, and cast them down.

"I am still chained, but as the House falls, my strength will grow, and my prison will weaken. In time, I will be free, or so these flowers promise me. I have been stripping the petals to throw upon my enemies. The puppets do not like it, for they know the flowers are a harbinger of change. Go, I grant you the time to look upon them!"

Arthur stood up nervously and looked across the clock face, but he didn't move. He didn't really want to go anywhere near the trapdoors on either side of the central pivot of the clock.

"Hurry," urged the Old One.

Arthur walked closer. The trapdoors were smashed in, splintered stubs of timber hanging from the thick iron hinges. Something rustled from inside, and Arthur looked down into a deep narrow chamber that was piled high with rose petals. The puppet woodchopper was there, still with its green cap on, the feather bent in half. But its limbs were broken, and all it could do was wriggle on the rose petals, gnash its teeth, and hiss.

Arthur shuddered and retreated to the rim, almost backing into the Old One.

"I hope . . . I hope we will not be enemies," said Arthur.

The Old One inclined his head, but did not speak. Arthur jumped down from the clock face and hurried away, his mind churning with fears and facts and suppositions. He had hoped the Old One could help him make sense of his situation, make matters clearer.

But he had only made it worse.

Chapter Five

"Lord Arthur, I am vastly relieved to see you," called out Scamandros as he saw Arthur hurrying back. "I trust the Old One answered your questions?"

"Not exactly," said Arthur. "Not even close, really. Is the Nothing still advancing?"

In answer, Scamandros cast out a lure with his fishing rod. The lure, a lobsterlike crustacean four or five inches long, disappeared into darkness. Scamandros wound the line back in, counting marks on the woven thread as he did so. There was no lure on the end.

"Six . . . seven . . . eight. The speed of encroachment has increased, Lord Arthur."

"Where was Dame Primus when you last were in touch? And Suzy?"

"They were both in the Citadel," said Scamandros. "It has become the general headquarters of your forces throughout the House, Lord Arthur."

"Could be tricky to get there," said Arthur. "Using the Fifth Key, I mean, since they secured the Citadel against Lady Friday. I suppose we could take the Improbable

Stair —" Scamandros began to shake his head, and Arthur stopped himself. "Oh, yeah, you can't go on the Stair. Oh, well . . . there was a mirror in Sir Thursday's . . . in my quarters. I guess I can try that, and if it doesn't work then we'll have to think of somewhere else, in the Middle House or wherever, and try to take an elevator from there."

He took out the Fifth Key and held it up for a moment in front of his face, then dropped it to his side.

"Uh, if I can make a door, how do I take you with me?"

Dr. Scamandros held up his hand and wiggled his fingers.

"If you allow me to hold on to your coattails, I shall be carried through, Lord Arthur."

"Hold on, then," said Arthur. "We'll give it a try."

He looked into the mirror and tried to remember what his quarters in Thursday's Citadel had looked like. He remembered the big four-poster bed with the carved battle scenes on the posts, and then there was the wardrobe, the chair he'd been shaved in, and, yes, there was a tall, bronze-framed mirror in the corner. If he thought of that mirror like a window, then looking through it he would be able to see the bed, and the door, and the painting on the wall . . .

Slowly, he began to see the room, though much of it was clouded and fuzzy. It took him a few seconds to work out that the bronze mirror was partially covered with a cloth. But he could see enough of the chamber, he was sure, for the Key to open a door there.

"Fifth Key, take me . . . us . . . to my room in the Citadel of the Great Maze!"

It was not so easy to go through the door of white light this time, nor was the transfer so immediate. Arthur felt himself held back not just by his coattails but by a force that pushed against his entire body and tried to throw him back. He struggled against it, with mind and body, but it was like walking against a very powerful wind. Then all of a sudden it was gone. He fell into his room in the Citadel, and Dr. Scamandros fell over his legs. Both of them tumbled across the floor, and Arthur hit his head against the carved battle scenes on the left-hand post of the huge bed.

"Ow!" he exclaimed. He felt his head, but there was no blood, and after a moment the sharp pain reduced to a dull ache.

"I do beg your pardon, Lord Arthur," said Dr. Scamandros as he got to his feet. "Most clumsy of me. That was fascinating — quite a different experience than a transfer plate. I am enormously grateful to you for saving me from the Deep Coal Cellar."

Arthur stood, using the bedpost to haul himself upright. As he did so, the sleeves of his paper coat rode up. He slid them back down, and for the first time noticed that they finished well short of his wrists. His trousers were also now ridiculously short, real ankle-freezers.

"I'd better get changed," Arthur said. He started toward the walk-in wardrobe, hesitated, and went back to the door, throwing it open to shout, "Sentry!"

A startled Denizen in the uniform of a Horde Troop Sergeant hurtled into the room and stood quivering at attention, his lightning tulwar crackling as he saluted with it. Arthur heard the crash of at least a dozen boots out of sight down the corridor, evidence of more troopers suddenly coming from rest to parade-ground attention.

"Lord Arthur! Guard present, sir!"

Arthur was already in the wardrobe, taking off his paper clothes and quickly putting on the plainest uniform he could find, which happened to be the sand-colored tunic and matching pale yellow leather breeches of a Borderer on desert duty, though this particular tunic had gold braid stitched across the shoulders and the leather breeches had gold stripes down each leg. Both tunic and breeches were much softer and more comfortable than anything a regular Borderer would ever be lucky enough to wear. They fit perfectly after a moment, shifting and altering themselves from Sir Thursday's size to Arthur's new height and musculature.

"Thank you!" Arthur called out to the sergeant. "We'll go down to the operations room in a minute. Is Dame Primus here? And Suzy Turquoise Blue?

"Dame Primus is in the operations room, sir!" boomed the Troop Sergeant. He appeared to be under the impression that Arthur was either deaf or much farther away than he actually was. "General Turquoise Blue is somewhere in the Citadel."

"General Turquoise Blue?" asked Arthur. "I didn't make Suzy a general, did I? I remember her talking about it, but I don't remember actually . . ."

"She probably just put on the uniform," said Dr. Scamandros. "No one would question her."

Arthur frowned, but the frown quickly gave way to laughter.

"That sounds like Suzy," he said. "I bet she did it to get a better grade of tea or something. Or to annoy Dame Primus."

He picked up a pair of armored sandals, looked at them for a moment, then dropped them back on the shelf and chose a pair of plain, but glossy, black boots instead.

"It's good to have you back, sir," said the Troop Sergeant as Arthur strode out of the wardrobe.

"Thank you again, Sergeant," said Arthur. "Let's get

to the operations room. I need to find out exactly what's going on."

There were at least twenty guards in the corridor, who formed up around Arthur as soon as he appeared. As they all marched together to the operations room, Arthur asked the guard commander to also send a messenger to find Suzy.

The operations room had grown larger in the few days of House time that had passed since Arthur had been there last. It was still a large domed chamber, but the walls had been pushed back to make it twice the size it had been before. It was now as big as his school's gymnasium, and in addition to all the soldiers in the various uniforms of the Regiment, the Horde, the Legion, the Moderately Honorable Artillery Company, and the Borderers, there were also numerous Denizens in civilian attire, many of them with their coats off and the sleeves of their white shirts covered with green ink-protectors up to the elbow.

Besides the central map table, which was also much longer and broader than it had been, there were now rows and rows of narrow, student-style desks for the civilians, who were all busy talking on old-fashioned phones or scribbling down messages. Every few seconds one would push his or her chair back and race across the room with a message slip, going either to Marshals Dawn, Noon, or Dusk, or to Dame Primus, who loomed over the map table, looking intently at various details while many Denizens babbled out messages around her, often at the same time.

Dame Primus was even taller than ever, perhaps eight and a half feet from toe to crown. She was wearing an armored hauberk of golden scales that clattered as she moved. The whole outfit looked decidedly uncomfortable, and dangerous for others, as it was ornamented with spiked pauldrons made to look like gripping claws. Even though the points of the claws gripped her shoulders, they also had spurs and flanges poking out in all directions.

The gauntlets that comprised the Second Key were folded through Dame Primus's broad leather belt, next to the buckle. The clock-hand sword of the First Key hung scabbarded at her left hip. The small trident that was the Third Key sat in its holster on her right hip, and she held the marshal's baton that was the Fourth Key, occasionally gesturing with it.

The cacophony of shouted messages, ringing telephones, scraping chairs, and clattering, hobnailed, or leather-soled Denizens suddenly ceased as Arthur's presence was announced. Then the noise redoubled as everyone in the room leaped from their chairs or pushed themselves off a wall, turned to the door, and came to attention.

"Carry on!" called Arthur immediately. There was just a moment's more silence, and then the room erupted into motion once more. The telephone earpieces rattled on their candlestick bodies as the old bells inside clattered more than rang, the messengers ran across the room, and the officers resumed talking all at once.

But the messengers did not get to deliver their hastily scrawled message forms to Dame Primus. She held up one hand and waved them back, striding across the room to greet Arthur with Marshals Dawn, Noon, and Dusk close behind her.

"Lord Arthur, a most timely arrival. I trust you have learned not to accept gifts from strange visitors?"

It took Arthur a moment to work out that Dame Primus was referring to the package he'd taken from Friday's servant Emelena, which had contained a Transfer Plate that had immediately activated, taking him to the Middle House. He had forgotten that he hadn't seen Dame Primus since then, or not all of her, at least. He'd found Part Five, who he quite liked and had hoped would round out the character of the Will, adding some much-needed common sense. Part Five had been assimilated, judging by what he had first assumed was a half-cloak on the back of Dame

Primus but now saw were in fact delicate semi-transparent gray wings that were very similar to those that had been on the bat-beast that had lurked in the Inner Darkness of the Middle House.

"I'll know better next time," he said. "What I need to know now is what's happening. Is the Lower House really destroyed?"

"Apart from the Deep Coal Cellar, the Lower House is entirely lost," Dame Primus confirmed. "As are the Far Reaches, and Nothing continues to surge against our defenses. Only the Keys can strengthen the fabric of the House, and we are threatened on too many fronts for me to deal with everything by myself. If you take the Fifth Key to the Middle House and reinforce the bulwark there, I will go to the Border Mountains here and build them up —"

"Hold on," interrupted Arthur. "How did this happen in the first place? And where is the Piper's Army? Are we still fighting Newniths here?"

"Really, Lord Arthur, there is no time to waste," said Dame Primus. "The Piper's Army has withdrawn and is no longer of immediate importance. Shoring up the foundations of the House is, and only you and I can do anything about that —"

"What about Superior Saturday?" asked Arthur. "What

is she up to? Why does she want the House to fall, and what are we going to do about her? I'm not going anywhere until you, or someone, tells me everything I want to know!"

Dame Primus loomed over him. Though he had gotten taller, she was far taller still, and her eyes were narrowed and her mouth was tight with displeasure. Arthur felt a strong urge to step back, even to kneel in awe of her terrible beauty and power. Instead he forced himself to take a step forward and look at her straight in her strange eyes, their pink irises surrounding pupils of intense darkness. She was every inch the embodiment of the Architect's Will, and Arthur knew that if he gave in to her now, he would never have the chance to make his own decisions ever again.

"I am the Rightful Heir, aren't I?" he said. "I want to know *exactly* what the situation is. Then *I* will decide what we are going to do."

Dame Primus met his gaze for a full second, then slowly inclined her head.

"Very well, Lord Arthur," she said. "As you command, so it shall be."

"Right, then," said Arthur. "First things first. What actually happened to the Lower House? Did Nothing break through in the Far Reaches?"

"I will show you, through the eyes of someone who was there." Dame Primus gestured with the baton, and all the lamps in the room suddenly dimmed. "Mister Skerrikim, I trust you still have the survivor?"

A Denizen in a dark frock coat, black cravat, and embroidered silver skullcap answered in the affirmative from the back of the room and made his way over to Dame Primus, lugging a large and rather battered leather suitcase fastened with three straps.

"An elevator operator was just closing his doors when it happened," said Dame Primus to Arthur. "He managed to get most of the way out of the Far Reaches before the Nothing caught him. By holding on to the ceiling light of the elevator with his teeth, his head and a small remnant of the elevator actually arrived here. Fortunately Mister Skerrikim was just in time to prevent his total dissolution."

Mr. Skerrikim, who Arthur had never seen before, laid the suitcase down on the floor, undid the straps, and opened it up. The case was full of rose petals, and in the middle of the petals lay a disembodied head swathed from temple to chin in clean white bandages, like an old-fashioned treatment for a toothache. The head had its eyes shut.

Mr. Skerrikim picked up the head by the ears and propped it against the open lid so it faced Arthur and Dame

Primus. Then he took a small bottle of activated ink out of his pocket, dipped a quill pen into it, and wrote something in extraordinarily tiny letters on the forehead of the survivor.

"Wake up, Marson!" instructed Mr. Skerrikim cheerfully.

Arthur started as the head's eyes flicked open. Dr. Scamandros, who was a step or two behind the boy, muttered something that did not sound very friendly.

"What is it?" Marson's head asked grumpily. "It's hard work growing a new body. Not to mention painful! I need all my rest."

"You shall have plenty of rest!" declared Mr. Skerrikim. "We're just going to have another look at what happened down that pit, near the dam wall."

"Must you?" asked Marson. The head's mouth quivered and tears formed in the corners of his eyes. "I just can't relive it again — the pain of the Nothing as it ate away my limbs —"

"This is entirely unnecessary!" protested Dr. Scamandros as he pushed past several interested officers to stand next to Arthur. The tattoos on his face were of painted savages dancing around a bonfire, under the direction of a witch doctor in a ludicrous feathered headdress. "This poor chap need not *feel* his immediate past merely for us to see it! I see also that you, sir, have used a quite discredited spell for the preservation of a head, and I must ask you to relinquish care of this individual to someone who knows what they are doing!"

"Mister Skerrikim is quite adequately trained," said Dame Primus smoothly. She did not look at Dr. Scamandros, but spoke to Arthur. "As Sir Thursday's Chief Questioner, Skerrikim has conducted many showings from Denizens' minds, and as you know, Arthur, Denizens do not really feel much pain. Marson will be well rewarded when his new body grows."

"I thought Doctor Scamandros was the only sorcerer not in Saturday's service," said Arthur.

"Mister Skerrikim is not exactly a sorcerer," Dame Primus clarified. "It is true he is a practitioner of House sorcery, but his field of specialization is quite narrow."

"Jackal," hissed Scamandros quietly.

"Blowhard," retorted Skerrikim, not so quietly.

Arthur hesitated. He wanted to see what Marson had experienced, but he didn't want the dismembered Denizen to suffer.

"Scamandros, can you show us what we need to see, without hurting him?"

"Indeed I can, sir," said Scamandros, puffing out his chest.

"Skerrikim is an expert," said Dame Primus. "Far better to let him —"

"No," Arthur said quietly. "Scamandros will do it. That will be all, thank you, Mister Skerrikim."

Skerrikim looked at Dame Primus. She did not move or give any signal that Arthur could see, but the skullcapped Denizen bowed and withdrew.

Scamandros knelt by the side of the suitcase and used a red velvet cloth to wipe off whatever Skerrikim had written on Marson's head. Then he took out his own bottle of activated ink and a peacock-plumed pen and wrote something else.

"Move aside," Scamandros instructed several officers. "The vision will form where you're standing. I trust you feel no pain, Marson?"

"Not a thing," Marson reported. "'Cept an itch in the foot I don't have anymore."

"Excellent," said Dr. Scamandros. "Open your eyes a little wider, a touch more . . . very good . . . hold them open there. . . . Let me get these matchsticks in place, and we will commence."

The sorcerer stood back and spoke a word. Arthur could almost see the letters of it, see the way the air rippled away from Scamandros's mouth as he spoke. He felt the power of the spell as a tingle in his joints, and some small part of him knew that once, long ago, he would have felt pain. Now, his body was accustomed to sorcery and used to power.

Two tiny pinpricks of light grew in Marson's eyes, and then two fierce beams shot forth, splaying out and gaining color, dancing around madly as if a crazed and manic artist were painting with streams of light.

An image formed in the air by the table, an image projected from Marson's propped-open eyes. A broad, cinematic view some twelve feet wide and eight feet high, it showed a part of the floor of the Pit in the Far Reaches, the great, deep hole that Grim Tuesday had dug in order to mine more and more Nothing, no matter how dangerous it was, and no matter how much it weakened the very foundations of the House.

Arthur leaned forward, intent on the scene. Even though what he was to see had already happened, he felt very tense, as if he were actually there. . . .

Chapter Six

"The memory is blurred," said Dame Primus. "We should have had Skerrikim do it."

"Merely a matter of focus, milady," said Scamandros. He bent down and adjusted Marson's eyelids, the shadows of his fingers walking across the lit scene like tall, dark walking trees. "There we are."

The picture became sharp, and sound came in as well. They were seeing what Marson had seen. The Denizen was looking out through the door of his elevator, his finger ready to press one of the bronze buttons that would take it up. Beyond the door, there was a rubble-strewn plain, lit here and there by an oil lamp hanging from an iron post. Some fifty yards away, a group of Denizens had gathered at the base of a great wall, a vast expanse of light gray concrete that had rods of shimmering iron protruding from it at regular intervals.

"Hey, that's the part I fixed up!" exclaimed Arthur. "With Immaterial-reinforced concrete."

The Denizens were looking at something. All of a

sudden they backed away, and one of them turned to call to someone out of sight.

"Sir! There's some sort of curious drill here! It's boring a hole all by itself! It's —"

Her words were cut off by a sudden, silent spray of Nothing that jetted out of the base of the wall. All the Denizens were cut down by it, instantly dissolved. Then more Nothing spewed out, and there was a terrible rumbling sound. Cracks suddenly ran from the ground up through the wall, cracks that began to bubble with dark Nothing.

A bell began to clang insistently and a steam whistle sounded a frantic scream.

Marson's finger jabbed a button. The doors began to close, even as a rolling wave of Nothing came straight at the elevator. His voice came through, loud and strange, heard through his own ears.

"No, no, no!"

He kept jabbing buttons. The doors shut and the elevator rocketed upward. Marson's fingers fumbled in his coat pocket, withdrawing a key that he used to quickly open a small hatch under the button panel. Inside was a red handle marked EMERGENCY RISE. Marson pulled it, a silk thread and wax seal snapping. The elevator gained speed, and he fell to his knees, but even the emergency rise was not fast enough. The floor of the elevator suddenly became as holed as a piece of Swiss cheese, blots of darkness eating it away. Marson leaped up and grabbed the chandelier in the ceiling, hauling himself up even as the lower half of the elevator disappeared. He was screaming and shrieking now, looking down at himself, where his legs had just ceased to exist —

"Stop!" said Arthur. "We've seen enough."

Scamandros snapped his fingers. The light from Marson's eyes faded. As the sorcerer bent down and removed the matchsticks, the disembodied head spoke.

"That weren't so bad."

"Thank you, Marson," said Arthur. He looked at Dame Primus. "I am sure you will be well looked after."

"As you see, Lord Arthur," said Dame Primus, "some kind of sabotage device of considerable power was used to breach the dam wall. It is likely that many other devices were employed at the same time, because almost the entire length of the dam wall fell at the same time. This allowed entry to a titanic surge of Nothing, which annihilated the Far Reaches in four or five minutes.

"Fortunately, the bulwark between the Far Reaches and the Lower House held for several hours, allowing enough time for the evacuation of important records and items, and a fair number of Denizens. Complete destruction of the Lower House followed, with the final remnants succumbing an hour ago. Nothing now presses directly against the lower bulwark of the Middle House.

"In a possibly unrelated complication, when the Piper's army withdrew, he covered his retreat with an explosion of Nothing that has weakened the barrier mountains here in the Great Maze, and, as always, there is Nothing leeching into the Border Sea. That is why we are both needed. We *must* use the power of the Keys to delay the destruction of the House."

"*Delay* the destruction?" asked Arthur. "Can't we stop it?"

"I doubt it. But we must hold off the Void long enough for you to claim the last two Keys. Then matters can be arranged in an orderly fashion."

"You mean that no matter what we do, the House — and the whole Universe beyond — is doomed?" asked Arthur. "It's only a matter of time?"

"I didn't say that, Lord Arthur." Dame Primus glanced away as she spoke, as if something had caught her eye. "You misunderstood me. Once we have stabilized the House, you can gain the Keys, and then we will be in a position to assess the damage and see what can be done."

"But I thought you said —"

"You misunderstood me," Dame Primus repeated

smoothly. She looked back at Arthur again and met his gaze. Even more than usual, he felt like a small animal caught in the glare of the headlights of a rapidly approaching truck, but he didn't look away. "Now, where do you wish to commence work? Here, with the mountains, or in the Middle House?"

"Neither," said Arthur. "Someone put those drills to work, and that someone pretty much has to be Superior Saturday, doesn't it? Or Lord Sunday, working with her, I suppose, though that bit of paper poor old Ugham had suggests otherwise."

"What paper?" Dame Primus asked suspiciously.

"The one signed just with an 'S' that said 'I do not wish to intervene or interfere' or whatever. It's in my old coat, I think."

"Signed merely with a single 'S'? That is Lord Sunday's mark. Superior Saturday, as she calls herself, would not be so humble as to use a single letter."

"Okay, that pretty much confirms Sunday's out of it — for now at least. So we need to make sure that Saturday can't do anything else. I mean, it's all very well shoring up the defenses, but what if she's undermining the House somewhere else we don't even know about?"

The three Marshals nodded in approval. Attack was the best method of defense, as far as they were concerned.

"I agree that Saturday must be dealt with," said Dame Primus. "But our first priority must be to reinforce the House! It is not supposed to fall like this. I cannot be in two places at once, so you have to do some of the work. When what we hold of the House is secure, then we can talk about freeing Part Six of myself and confronting Saturday. Not before!"

"You can't be in two places at once," said Arthur thoughtfully, almost to himself.

"I beg your pardon?" Dame Primus bent forward a little, as if to hear Arthur better.

"You can't be in two places at once," Arthur repeated loudly. "Yet we have five Keys between us, and once you were five separate beings. Is it possible for you to become two?"

Dame Primus frowned even more.

"I mean two of you, with an equal mix of all parts of the Will," Arthur added hurriedly. Most of the individual parts of the Will were quite unbalanced, some of them dangerously so. He didn't want the snaky, judgmental Part Four off on its own, for example.

"It . . . is . . . possible," said Dame Primus. "But not at all recommended. We would do much better —"

"And you can join back together again?" Arthur was not giving up on the idea so easily.

Dame Primus nodded stiffly.

"Okay, then you can split into two and each half of you can take two Keys and go fix up whatever needs fixing up," said Arthur. "Or, hey, you could split into four and take a Key each —"

"I will *not* divide myself so much," said Dame Primus furiously. "It would merely offer a target for Saturday or even the Piper, who might well overcome such a fraction of myself and wrest the Keys from our control."

"Two, then," said Arthur. "Dame Primus and Dame . . . uh . . . Two?"

"Secundus," whispered Scamandros.

"This is not a good idea, Arthur," said Dame Primus. "To lessen my power by half is foolish in the extreme. And if you think this will allow you to return to your Secondary Realm, then you have failed to consider your own transformation, and the effect you will have —"

"I'm not going back home," Arthur interrupted coldly. "At least not yet. Like I said, we need to deal with Superior Saturday. That means freeing Part Six of the Will to start with, so please tell me — do you know where it is? I know you can sense the other parts of yourself."

Dame Primus straightened up.

"Part Six of myself is definitely somewhere within the Upper House. I do not know where exactly, and I have no means of finding out. The Upper House has been closed to us by means of sorcery. No elevators go there now, there are no telephone connections, and the Front Door remains firmly shut. So once again, even if it was in our best interests for you to go there, it is not possible, and you would do better to help me and not make foolish — that is to say, *naive* — suggestions about me dividing myself."

"There's no way there at all?" asked Arthur. "What about the Improbable — no, I'd have to have visited there before. Same for the Fifth Key . . ."

"As I said, there is no way," Dame Primus insisted. "Once again illustrating that I know best, Arthur. You must remember that although you are the Rightful Heir, you were just a mortal boy not so long ago. No one can expect you to have the wisdom —"

Arthur ignored her. Another plan had just occurred to him. "There might be a way," he said. "I'll have to go and check it out."

"What?" asked Dame Primus, indignant. "What way? Even if you *could* get to the Upper House, you must remember that Saturday has thousands of sorcerers, perhaps even tens of thousands. Acting in concert and directed by her, they could easily overcome you, take you prisoner —"

"I'm not just going to charge in," said Arthur. He was getting increasingly tired of Dame Primus's objections. "In fact, if I can get there the way I'm thinking, it will be a very sneaky approach. Anyway, we're wasting time. You need to split into two, Dame Primus, and get to work. I have to head over to the Border Sea."

"This is all too hasty!" protested Dame Primus. "What can you possibly want in the Border Sea?"

"The Raised Rats."

Dame Primus took in an outraged breath and her frown got so deep, her eyebrows almost met in a huddle above her nose.

"The Raised Rats are agents of the Piper! Like the Piper's children, they are not to be trusted! They are to be hunted down and exterminated!"

"Old Primey got her undergarments in a twist again," said a voice behind him. He turned and smiled as he saw his friend Suzy Turquoise Blue expertly slide between two Denizens to stand next to him.

"Suzy! What on earth are you wearing?"

"M'uniform," said Suzy. She raised her battered top hat, which now had two oversize gold epaulettes sewn to the back like a sun-cape, and bowed. The half-dozen probably unearned medals on her red regimental coat (that had the sleeves cut off to show her yellow shirt) jangled as she made a bow, and the leg she thrust forward creaked, since she was also wearing the same kind of leather breeches as

Arthur, which he had thought were exclusive to Sir Thursday. Her boots were red and did not resemble those in any uniform that Arthur had learned about in his recruit training. Neither did the iridescent-green-scaled belt she wore, though the savage-sword at her side was in a regulation sheath.

Arthur blinked, not least because there were several other Piper's children clad in similar strange combinations standing behind Suzy.

"Suzy's Raiders," Suzy said, seeing him look. "Irregulars. Marshal Dusk signed off on it. Told 'im it was your idea."

"My idea," Arthur started to say, but he bit off his words as he saw Suzy wiggling her eyebrows at him.

"On account of the Piper's children bein' under a cloud, so to speak," added Suzy. "Better to 'ave us all in one lot. Easier to watch, that way. If Old Prim — I mean, if Dame Primus wants to knock us off."

"It's not a personal matter, Miss Blue," said Dame Primus with a sniff. "I am merely doing whatever is necessary to ensure Lord Arthur's eventual triumph. You yourself have fallen under the spell of the Piper's music once. Ensuring that it doesn't happen again is simply common sense."

"You don't have to kill us," said Suzy, bristling. She rummaged in her pockets and produced two ugly gray stumps of candle wax. "We can just stick this 'ere wax in our ears and we won't be able to hear the pipe! Besides, it's General Turquoise Blue now!"

Dame Primus snorted and was about to speak when Arthur held up his hand.

"I've already given orders that no Piper's children are to be harmed," he said. "Neither are the Raised Rats, provided they do not act against us. Now, I *am* going to see the Rats. They owe me a question, and I owe them an answer, so I'm sure they will at least negotiate. Dame Primus, Marshals, everyone, please carry on as we have discussed. Doctor Scamandros, would you mind coming with me?"

"Certainly, Lord Arthur, certainly," puffed Dr. Scamandros. "Ah, do you intend to use the Fifth Key again?"

"It's the quickest way," said Arthur. "I can go straight to the *Rattus Navis IV*. I can probably see out of the reflection of the silver jug they had. What, Suzy?"

Suzy was tugging at his sleeve.

"I'm coming too, right? To see the Rats and then sort out Saturday?"

"You probably should stay and look after the Piper's child —"

"Stay! Just because you've got taller than's sensible and your teeth all shined up doesn't mean you can do without me! Who's saved your bacon a mort of times?"

"I perhaps should advise you, Lord Arthur, that I felt quite a level of resistance when we traveled here," said Scamandros. "Indeed, I was almost hurled back. It might be more prudent to take the elevator to Port Wednesday and send for the Raised Rats."

"There isn't time," said Arthur. "But I think I will need you, so if you can bear it —"

"I will attend you," said Scamandros. "I will hold on more tightly this time, though you now lack coattails. If I may take your arm?"

"What about me?" Suzy demanded.

"Yes, you can come too," Arthur told her. "At least to talk to the Rats."

Arthur offered one arm to Dr. Scamandros and the other to Suzy, though this made it difficult to hold up the Fifth Key. He was about to gaze into it when he hesitated and looked across at Dame Primus. She had gone back to the map table and was studying it, giving no sign that she was about to split in two and do as he asked.

Arthur had also remembered something else.

"Dame Primus!" he called out. "Before you do split into two, I would like *The Compleat Atlas of the House* back again. I expect it will also be very useful."

Dame Primus kept looking at the table and did not turn her head to speak.

"The Atlas has a mind of its own," she said. "I believe it was last seen in the Middle House, probably getting a new binding put on without visible assistance. I expect it will return here in due course, or it will find you wherever you are. I suggest that you check any bookshelves you happen to be near."

"Oh," said Arthur, and then it struck him.

She's lying to me, he thought. *Or avoiding the truth. I wonder why she doesn't want me to have the Atlas? It could be very useful. But she can't look me in the eye and lie —*

Marshal Dawn erupted from her desk and rushed across the room, brandishing a message slip and calling, "Dame Primus! There is a small geyser of Nothing reported near Letterer's Lark!"

Dame Primus took the slip.

"You see, Arthur! Well, if you will not go, then I must do as you ask. Marshal Dawn, prepare an escort and the private elevator!"

Dawn saluted and rushed away. There was a hush in the room as everyone watched Dame Primus, a hush that immediately dissipated as she looked about her, a deep frown on her face. Frenetic activity resumed everywhere, apart from a quiet space around Dame Primus and another around Arthur, Suzy, and Scamandros.

"Reckon this'll be worth seeing," muttered Suzy. "Think she'll split in half and wriggle like a worm?"

Arthur shook his head. That would be too undignified for Dame Primus.

As they watched, she took a step forward, and as she did so, she blurred and diminished, as if she'd walked into a hole in the ground. Then a smaller version of herself walked ahead, leaving a second smaller version behind, so that there were two seven-foot-tall Dame Primuses standing in a line, instead of one eight-foot-plus version. They looked identical and were dressed exactly the same, but one had the clock-sword of the First Key and the trident of the Third Key, and the other had the gauntlets of the Second Key and the baton of the Fourth.

The two embodiments of the Will turned to each other and curtsied.

"Dame Quarto," said the one who had the sword and the gauntlets.

"Dame Septum," said the one who had the trident and the baton.

"Hmmph," whispered Scamandros. "Self-aggrandizement. They've added one and three, and two and five. Trying to make the sum of the whole greater, I suppose."

Quarto and Septum turned and curtsied to Arthur.

"Lord Arthur," they chorused.

"Hello," said Arthur. "Thank you for splitting. I guess we'd all better get on with it."

"Indeed," said Dame Quarto.

"We had," added Dame Septum. She raised her hand and dramatically announced, "I shall attend to the Middle House!"

"And I to the mountains!" declared Dame Quarto, and both strode from the room.

"And I to ... sorting out Superior Saturday," said Arthur. Somehow it didn't sound the same. He raised the mirror and concentrated on looking through it and out of the reflection in the silver jug in the stern cabin of the *Rattus Navis IV.* He would soon find himself wherever the ship might be upon the strange waters of the Border Sea.

Chapter Seven

It was much harder going through the doorway with two people hanging on, and for a fearful moment Arthur thought all three of them would be thrown back, and not to the safety of the Citadel, but somewhere else not of his choosing. The ground swayed unsteadily beneath his feet, the light dazzled his eyes, and Suzy and Scamandros felt like enormous lead weights dragging his arms back and down. But he kept pushing forward, his total concentration on reaching his goal. He could half-see the table and chairs in the big cabin on the *Rattus Navis IV*. Even though it looked just a step away, it was almost impossible to reach.

Then, with a Herculean effort that left Arthur sweating and gasping, they fell out onto the tilted-over floor of the ship and slid across the floorboards into the starboard hull. Then, as the ship rolled back the other way and pitched forward, they slid diagonally across to the port side, smacked into the table, and sent the silver jug clanging onto the deck.

As they got up and grabbed hold of whatever they

could to stay upright, the door burst open and a Newnith soldier gaped in the doorway.

"Boarders!" he shouted as he drew a sparking dagger from the sheath at his belt. "The enemy!"

Scamandros reached into his sleeve and came out with a tiny cocktail fork with a pickled onion on it, which he didn't expect and hurriedly replaced.

Suzy drew her savage-sword at the same time, but the Newnith was quicker and had his sea legs. He rushed at Arthur, who instinctively raised his arm to protect himself, even though an arm would be no real protection from a long dagger that was spewing out white-hot sparks.

But it was his right arm, and in his right hand Arthur held the Fifth Key. Before the Newnith could fully complete his downward cut at the boy, there was a brilliant flash of light, a sudden, strange chemical stench, a stifled scream, and then just a pair of smoking boots on the deck where the Newnith had been.

Arthur felt a surge of annoyance.

How dare these pathetic creatures attack me? he thought. *How dare they! I shall walk among them and wreak havoc. . . .*

Arthur shook his head and took a breath, forcing this arrogant temper tantrum back to wherever it had come from. He was frightened by it, frightened that he could get so angry, and that his immediate response was to attack.

As the rage lessened, he became aware that his arm hurt quite a lot.

"Ouch!" he exclaimed. The point of the Newnith's dagger had made contact with him after all. He rolled his arm over to get a better look, and saw that it had done more than just scratch the skin. There was a six-inch-long incision in his forearm, and it looked cut to the bone. Yet even as he looked, the cut closed up, leaving only a very faint white scar. Arthur wiped off what little blood there was with his left hand, and tried not to notice that it was neither red like a normal human's nor blue like a Denizen's. It was golden, like a deep, rich honey, and that was almost more painful to him than the cut itself. Whatever he was becoming was very strange indeed.

"There's nothing left of 'im," said Suzy with satisfaction, turning over the vaporized Newnith's smoking boots with the point of her sword.

"I didn't mean to do it," said Arthur sadly. "It was the Key."

"We'd best get ready." Suzy tugged on the table, to drag it to the door, but it was bolted to the deck and she only succeeded in staggering into Scamandros when she lost her grip. Still unsteady, both of them went backwards into one of the well-upholstered chairs. Suzy was up again in a moment, while Scamandros struggled like a beetle thrown upon its back.

"Won't just be one Newnith on board," Suzy warned. "They'll be charging in any moment."

"They might not have heard," said Arthur. It *was* noisy, the constant rhythmic thud of the ship's steam engine mixed with the groan and creak of the rigging above, as well as the regular crash and jolt as the ship plunged through what had to be fairly sizable waves.

"They heard orright," said Suzy. She spat on her hands and gripped her sword more tightly. "I expect your Key can burn up a passel of 'em, though."

"I don't want to burn them up," Arthur protested. "I just want to talk to the Raised Rats!"

"We are very glad to hear that," said a voice from under the table.

Suzy swore and ducked down to have a look.

"A trapdoor," she exclaimed in admiration. "Sneaky!"

A four-foot-tall rat clad in white breeches and a blue coat with a single gold epaulette on his left shoulder clambered out from under the table and saluted Arthur, his long mouth open in a smile that revealed two shiny gold-capped front teeth. He had a cutlass at his side, but it was sheathed. A Napoleonic hat perched at a jaunty angle on his head.

"Lord Arthur, I presume? I am Lieutenant Goldbite, recently appointed to command this vessel following Captain Longtayle's promotion and transfer. I didn't have the pleasure of meeting you before, but I am acquainted with your past dealings with us. Perhaps you and your companions would like to sit?"

He gestured at the armchairs.

"Do we have a truce?" asked Arthur, still standing. "And do you speak for all aboard?"

"I am the captain," said Goldbite. "I say truce for all of us, Newniths and Raised Rats."

"The Piper's not 'ere, is he?" asked Suzy. She hadn't sat down either, though Scamandros had settled back down only moments after finally managing to get up.

"The Piper is not aboard this ship," said Goldbite. "And though we owe him a considerable debt and so will carry his troops and so forth, the Raised Rats have chosen to be noncombatants in the Piper's wars, and should not be considered in the same light as the Newniths. Speaking of them, if you wouldn't mind sitting down, I shall just pop out and stand down both my own folk and the Newniths."

"I'm sorry about the one . . . the one I killed," said Arthur. He was very aware that the Newniths, though they felt obliged to serve the Piper, actually just wanted to be farmers. Arthur felt they were much more like humans than Denizens. "He attacked me, and the Key . . ."

Goldbite nodded. "I will tell them. He was not the first, nor will he be the last. But I trust there will be no more fighting between us on the *Rattus Navis IV*. Please do help yourself to biscuits from that tin there, and there is more cranberry juice in the keg."

"Might as well," said Arthur as the Raised Rat left via the door. He picked up the silver jug and refilled it from the keg, while Suzy got out the biscuits, tapping them on the table to make the weevils fall out. She offered them around, but Arthur and Scamandros passed, the latter taking a slightly crushed ham and watercress sandwich on a red checkered china plate out of one of his inner pockets.

"I'm curious to know why there are Newniths on board," said Arthur quietly. "I hope the Piper isn't going to attack us here in the Border Sea."

"Port Wednesday is well defended," said Dr. Scamandros. "The Triangle would be more at risk, if none of the regular vessels are there to protect it. But there would be little to gain from taking that, since it has no elevators or anything very useful. But of course the Rats could be taking the Newniths elsewhere by way of the Border Sea, out into the Secondary Realms —"

"Ssshhh," Arthur hushed. "Goldbite's coming back."

Goldbite knocked and then poked his long nose around the door.

"All settled in?" he asked before coming in. "Very good. I'm afraid my First Lieutenant can't join us, as she has the watch, but my Acting Third Lieutenant will do so. I believe you have already met."

The Raised Rat behind Goldbite stepped out and saluted. Though his whiskers had been trimmed and he wore a blue coat, Arthur recognized him immediately.

"Watkingle! You've been promoted!"

"Yes, sir," said Watkingle. "And it was for hitting you on the head, sir, and averting a disastrosphe or cataster, whichever you like. That was a good hit for me, if you don't mind me saying so, sir."

"I don't mind — it was needed at the time." Arthur got up and shook Watkingle's paw. "Feverfew would have had me, otherwise."

"You're looking . . . uh . . . well, sir," said Watkingle. "Taller."

"Yes," replied Arthur, not very happily. He sat back

down. Watkingle lounged back against the hull, bracing his paws so that he was not thrown off balance by the pitch and roll of the ship.

"I take it you have come to ask your third question?" said Goldbite, after the ensuing silence started to feel uncomfortable.

"Well, both a question and a request for aid," Arthur replied. "I hear that Superior Saturday has completely cut off the Upper House, and that there is no way to get there. But I bet you Rats know a way. In fact, I know you must, because a Raised Rat managed to get out with a piece of paper. I want to find out what that way is, and I want you to help me get there."

"And me!" added Suzy.

"Hmmm," said Goldbite. "I shall have to send a message to Commodore Monckton —"

Arthur shook his head.

"There's no time. I presume you know that the Nothing defenses in the Far Reaches were sabotaged and the dam wall was destroyed. The Lower House has also been destroyed. I have to stop Saturday before she manages to destroy the entire House."

Goldbite wrinkled his nose in agitation.

"We had news of a disaster, but did not know it was so extreme," he said. "But to answer your question, I must reveal secrets. I've not been in command of this vessel long, nor am I very senior. . . ."

"I have already ordered the Raised Rats to be left alone unless they act against my forces," said Arthur. "I'm happy to do anything I can for you, and to answer any number of questions, if you can tell me how to get into the Upper House." He paused and then corrected, "How to get into the Upper House without being noticed, that is."

"As you have guessed, Lord Arthur, there *is* a way," said Goldbite slowly. He looked at Watkingle, who shrugged. "All things considered, I believe I must assist you. But you must agree to a price to be set by Commodore Monckton and those Rats senior to me, in addition to the answer you already owe us."

"That's a pig in a poke," said Suzy. "You Rats really take the biscuit."

"Why, thank you," said Watkingle. He leaned forward and took a biscuit.

"That's not what I meant!" protested Suzy. "Why should Arthur agree to —"

"It's okay, Suzy," said Arthur. "I do agree."

If I don't agree, it soon won't matter, he figured. And a small voice inside him, a deep and nasty part of his mind, added, *Besides, I can go back on my word. They're only Rats. . . .*

"I must also ask you to keep this secret, Lord Arthur," continued Goldbite. "All of you must keep it secret."

Arthur nodded, as did Suzy, though he had a suspicion she'd crossed her fingers behind her back.

"Always happy to keep a secret," said Scamandros. "Got hundreds of them already, locked up here."

The sorcerer tapped his forehead, and a tattoo of a keyhole appeared there, a key went in and turned, and then both transformed into a spray of question marks that danced over his temples to his ears.

"Very well," said Goldbite. "Lord Arthur, you know about our Simultaneous Bottles, how something put in one bottle of a matched pair will appear in the other bottle?"

"Yes. For messages and so on. But Monckton told me they only work in the Border Sea!"

"That is true for most of them. But we do have a small number of very special Simultaneous Bottles, or, to be accurate, Simultaneous Nebuchadnezzars that not only work outside the Border Sea —"

"What's a Nebuchadnezzar?" asked Suzy.

"Size of bottle," said Scamandros. Eight bottles of increasing size appeared on his left cheek and spread across to his right cheek. The smallest was about half an inch high, the largest began at his chin and went to the top of his ear. "Big one. There's your ordinary bottle. Then comes a Magnum — that's two bottles' worth. Then a Jeroboam — that holds the same as four of the regular size. And so forth: Rehoboam, six bottles; Methuselah, eight; Salmanazar, twelve; Balthazar, sixteen; Nebuchadnezzar, twenty!"

He started to rummage inside his coat and added, "Got a Jeroboam of quite a nice little sparkling wine here somewhere, a gift from poor old Captain Catapillow —"

"Yes, yes," broke in Goldbite. "The Simultaneous Nebuchadnezzars are very large bottles that we have twinned in various locations about the House, including one in the Upper House. Their size is important because they are large enough to allow the transfer of one of us. But not, I hasten to say, someone of your size, Lord Arthur."

"I thought it might be something like that," said Arthur. "That's where you come in, Doctor Scamandros. I want you to turn me into a Raised Rat. Temporarily, that is."

"And me," said Suzy.

"It is not an easy thing to do," Dr. Scamandros warned. "It is true I once created illusions for you, to give you the appearance of rats. Actually reshaping you, even for a limited time — I don't know. You could do it yourself with the Key, Arthur."

Arthur nodded. "I probably could. But I would be worried about turning back again. But if you do it, it will wear off, won't it?"

"I should expect so," said Scamandros. "But I cannot be sure how any spell will affect you, Lord Arthur. It is possible the Key might perceive such a spell as an attack, and do the same thing to me that it did to that Newnith."

"I'm sure it wouldn't if I was concentrating on wanting to turn into a Raised Rat," said Arthur. "Anyway, let's give it a try."

Goldbite coughed and raised a paw.

"The Simultaneous Nebuchadnezzar that is twinned with the one we have secreted in the Upper House is not aboard this vessel. Should you wish to try it, upon the terms I have outlined, we must rendezvous with the *Rattus Navis II*. If I send a message and she steams towards us, and we to her, it should only be a matter of half an hour. We have been traveling in convoy."

"Convoy?" asked Arthur. "With loads of Newniths aboard? I hope you're not planning to attack Port Wednesday after all?"

"I do not know the ultimate destination of the Newnith force," answered Goldbite. "But I can tell you that we took them aboard in the Secondary Realms, and so I expect we shall disembark them in another."

"Okay, good," said Arthur. "I think. What can they be up to? I wish the Piper would just stay out of everything. I suppose I could ask one of the Newniths —"

"Please!" interrupted Goldbite. "As I said, the Raised Rats seek to be noncombatants. At present the Newniths have agreed to the polite fiction that one of their number was lost in an accident at sea. They will not come below to seek you out, but should you make yourself known, then they will feel compelled to fight. I expect you would win, Lord Arthur, but your companions could be killed, and certainly many Newniths would die. Please stay here, drink cranberry juice, and when we have made our rendezvous, we will transfer you to the other ship as quickly and quietly as is possible."

"All right." Once again Arthur had to fight back the urge to stride out upon the deck and order the Newniths to bow before him. And if they would not, then he would blast them to cinders and let wind and wave blow them away. . . .

No, thought Arthur. *Stop! I will do this my way. No matter what I look like on the outside, I am not going to change who I truly am. I am human and I know how to love, and be kind, and be compassionate to those who are weaker than me. Just because I have power doesn't mean I have to use it!*

"I am going to need some things," announced Dr. Scamandros, who was rummaging in his pockets. "Hmm . . . freshly cut Rat hair . . . four paw prints in jelly or plaster or sand, at a pinch . . . gray or brown paint, a bigger brush than this one . . . I think I have everything else."

"Watkingle can organize those items for you," said Goldbite.

"Whose fresh-cut Rat hair, sir?" asked Watkingle. "I ain't due for a haircut —"

"Someone will need one," said Goldbite. "See to it at once."

"Aye, aye," grumbled Watkingle. He left the cabin, mumbling to himself, "Hair, plaster, gray or brown paint . . ."

"Let me see," continued Dr. Scamandros. He set a green crystal bottle stoppered with a lead seal on the table. "The large bottle of activated ink . . . might be best to read up a little. There's that piece in *Xamanader's Xenographical Xactions* . . . sure I had a copy somewhere . . ."

"Where is the other Nebuchadnezzar? The one in the Upper House?" asked Arthur, though as always he was fascinated by the amount and size of the stuff Scamandros could keep in his coat. "And are there Rats who might be able to help me there?"

"I don't know much," replied Goldbite. "I believe it is in the very lowest levels of the Upper House, by the steam engines that drive the chains. We do have some agents in place. And, of course, the Piper's children there who help us would probably assist you too."

"Piper's children?" asked Suzy. "I never knew there was a bunch of us lot in the Upper House."

At the same time, Arthur asked, "Steam engines? Chains?"

Goldbite explained what little he could, with Scamandros interrupting a little, in between cataloging items he needed and re-sorting strange things that had come out of his coat. As it happened, the sorcerer could add little to Goldbite's explanations. Scamandros had been expelled from the Upper House several thousand years previously, and back then Superior Saturday had still used more conventional means to build her tower, and there had been other buildings too, not just one enormous, sprawling construction of iron cubes.

"It sounds like some sort of giant toy construction set," said Arthur. "And all the cubes get moved along rails by steam-driven chains?"

"So I am told," said Goldbite.

"Reckon that'll be worth looking at," said Suzy

happily. "Nothin' like a nice cloud of honest steam and a bit of sooty coal smoke to invigilate the lungs."

"Vigorate," said Scamandros absently. "In-vig-o-rate. The other's to do with exams and looking into matters. Cause of my downfall."

"I'm sure it will look interesting enough," said Arthur. "But we have to remember it's the fortress of our enemy. If you do come, Suzy, you have to stay out of sight and be sneaky. I don't want to have to fight thousands of sorcerers. Or Saturday, for that matter — not in her own demesne with the Sixth Key. We'll just go in, find Part Six of the Will, get it, and get out. Get it?"

"Got it," said Suzy.

"Good," said Arthur. At that moment, a fleeting memory of his father, Bob, flashed through his head, of him watching one of his favorite Danny Kaye films and laughing, fit to burst. But then it was gone, and Arthur couldn't think why it had come to mind. He wished he could have held on to it longer. His father, and his family, felt so distant. Even a brief memory of them made him feel not so much alone.

Chapter Eight

They were taken in a ship's boat from the *Rattus Navis IV* to the *Rattus Navis II*. Rowed by eight salty Rats with blue ribbons trailing from their straw hats who kept in time to Watkingle's hoarse roars of "Pull, Pull," the boat made a quick passage across the few hundred yards of open sea that separated the ships.

Arthur sat with his back against the bow, looking at the *Rattus Navis IV* and the ranks of Newniths on the deck. They were all facing the other way, studiously ignoring the departure of their brief fellow passenger. He was thinking about them, and where they might be going, and also thinking about where he was going, when a great spray of cold seawater splashed across his shoulders. He turned around just in time to cop the last of it in his open mouth, and saw that they were plunging down the face of a wave, having just cut through the crest of it, in the process taking on perhaps a third of a bucket of water. It would have been much more, save for Watkingle's skill in steering the boat.

In that small amount of water, which had mostly fallen over Arthur, there was something else, which now lay wet and sodden in his lap. It was a fluffy yellow elephant — his toy elephant, which he'd already found once in the Border Sea, home of lost things, only to lose it again somewhere between the Sea and the Great Maze.

"Elephant," he said dumbly, and clutched it to his chest, as tightly as he'd ever held it as a small child. Then he remembered who and where he was, and slowly lowered the toy back into his lap.

"You need to be careful with that," said Dr. Scamandros, looking at him over the top of his open copy of *Xamanader's Xenographical Xactions,* a small scarlet-colored book that looked too slim to have much sorcerous wisdom in it. "Childhood totems are very potent. Someone could make a Cocigrue from it, like the Skinless Boy, or perhaps a sympathetic needle to bring you pain."

"I won't lose Elephant again," said Arthur. He put the small toy inside his tunic and made sure it couldn't fall out. It made rather a strange lump, but he didn't care.

"I 'ad a toy when I was little," said Suzy. She frowned for a moment, then added, "Can't remember what it was. It moved and made me laugh. . . ."

"Ahoy the boat! Come alongside!"

Suzy's recollections were left behind as they scrambled up the rope ladder to the deck of the *Rattus Navis II,* where they were met by a nattily dressed Raised Rat whose uniform was much finer and considerably more decorative than any other Arthur had seen. Even the basic blue material of his coat had a swirling, silken pattern that caught the light.

"Greetings, Lord Arthur! I am Lieutenant Finewhisker, commander of this vessel. Please, come below. We have our own small contingent of Newniths aboard, senior officers for the most part, who have been kind enough to foregather in the bow and take tea while you . . . ahem . . . visit."

"Thank you," said Arthur.

"Follow me, please." Finewhisker moved quickly to the aft companionway and ushered them down to the captain's great cabin. It was similar to the cabin in the *Rattus Navis IV,* but was much more elaborately decorated. There were red velvet curtains on the windows, and the chairs were upholstered in a bright patterned cloth that looked almost like a tartan.

Arthur hardly noticed the decorations. The cabin was dominated by an enormous green glass bottle that sat in a wooden cradle that was lashed to the deck. The bottle was at least eight feet long and five feet in diameter, and if it wasn't for the neck being only as thick as his leg, he could have easily gotten inside *without* being turned into a Rat first.

The green glass was cloudy, but not entirely opaque, and something that looked like smoke or fog was swirling about inside, prevented from issuing out into the cabin by the Simultaneous Nebuchadnezzar's huge, wire-wrapped, steel-bonneted cork.

"Everything is prepared," said Finewhisker. "You need only enter the bottle, whenever you are ... ah ... made ready to do so. May I offer you a refreshing cordial, Lord Arthur, while your sorcerer prepares his spell?"

"No, thank you," said Arthur. "How long will it take you, Doctor Scamandros?"

Scamandros was sorting out his various supplies on the bench. He glanced over at Arthur, blinked several times at the Nebuchadnezzar, and coughed.

"Perhaps thirty minutes, Lord Arthur. If I may prevail upon someone to fetch me a large piece of cheese with the rind on, I would be grateful. I thought I had a slab of Old Chewsome, but I can't lay my hand on it."

"I will have the cook deliver some," Finewhisker said. "Please make yourselves comfortable. I must go on deck for a few minutes, but I will be back in plenty of time to open the Nebuchadnezzar. Quite a specialized technique is required, so please do not attempt the cork yourselves. I should also warn you not to touch the glass. The exterior of the bottle is often very, very cold, and occasionally very, very hot. As neither the heat nor cold radiates, it can be a very unpleasant shock."

"Doesn't radiate?" muttered Scamandros. "How very interesting."

He turned away from the plaster Rat footprints he had been holding and took a step toward the Nebuchadnezzar, then threw his hands up and turned back, the tattoo of a spinning ship's wheel on his forehead indicating that he had recalled his immediate task.

"So we go through this 'ere bottle," said Suzy thoughtfully. "Then we find Part Six of the Will, right?"

"Yes," said Arthur.

"'Ow exactly do we do that?" asked Suzy. "Reckon it might turn up like Part One and jump in me gob?"

"I wish it would," said Arthur. "But it will be trapped somehow. I'm hoping that I'll be able to feel its presence — I can kind of sense the Parts of the Will now. Or maybe it will be able to speak into my mind, as the other Parts did when I got close enough."

"I get a stomachache when Dame Primus is around," said Suzy. "Maybe that'll help."

"Anything might help. We'll have to be very careful. Presuming we can find and free Part Six, we'll use the Fifth Key to head straight back to the Citadel —"

"Oh, no, no, no," interrupted Scamandros. "You daren't do that! Didn't I explain? There's always a working of sorcerers watching for sorcery in the Upper House. I daresay there's even more of them than ever, these days. As soon as you start to use a Key, they'll hit you with a confinement or encyst you —"

"They will not dare cast a spell against the Rightful Heir, wielder of the Fifth Key!" pronounced Arthur, in stentorian tones. He stood up and thumped his chest. "They are mere Denizens, it is I who —"

He stopped, wiped his suddenly sweating forehead, and sat down.

"Sorry," he said, in his normal voice. "The Keys . . . they're working on me. So how do we get out once we have Part Six, Doctor?"

"I don't know, Lord Arthur," said Scamandros. "I am not much of a strategizer . . . all I know is that if you use a Key, you will have only moments before they act against you. If you are very swift, you might be able to get out before they land a spell on you. And it is possible you might be too strong, even for hundreds or thousands of

Saturday's sorcerers. But if they can hold you for a few minutes, that would be enough for Saturday herself to join the working."

"And the Sixth Key is strongest in its own demesne," said Arthur. "What does getting encysted mean, by the way?"

Scamandros shuddered and his tattoos turned a sickly green.

"You get turned inside out and trapped inside a . . . kind of bag . . . made out of your own bodily fluids . . . which are then vitrified, like glass."

"That's awful! If that happened, wouldn't I be dead?"

"Not if you're a Denizen. They can survive being encysted for a few months, maybe a year. Saturday used to have the cysts hung up here and there, as a warning. It was quite a rare punishment in my day."

"Sounds better than a hanging," said Suzy brightly. Then she frowned and added, "Only I can't remember any hangings. We used to go to them, and my mum'd take our nuncheon wrapped up in a white cloth. . . ."

Her voice trailed off as she tried to recall her long-ago human life.

"I will also have to give you something to wrap the Fifth Key in," Scamandros continued. "To hide its sorcerous emanations. I have just the thing, somewhere . . . but first I must finish constructing this spell. If you would both be so kind as to remain totally silent and look the other way for a few minutes, I need complete concentration."

Arthur and Suzy complied. Arthur twitched one of the fine curtains aside and looked out at the rolling sea. The waves came almost to the window, and spray splashed across every time the ship heeled over. But it was a tight window and didn't leak. Arthur found it quite hypnotic just watching the mass of moving gray-green water topped with white. For a few minutes he could empty his mind of all his troubles and just watch the endless sea. . . .

"Done!" exclaimed Scamandros.

Arthur and Suzy turned back. The plaster footprints and the Rat hair had disappeared and the bottle of activated ink was empty. Scamandros was holding the tin of gray paint in one hand and the large brush in the other.

"Right, clothes off. I've got to get you painted up."

Suzy took off her battered hat and started unbuttoning her coat.

"Hang on, uh, wait a moment." Arthur's cheeks colored with embarrassment. He'd gotten used to mixed washrooms in the Glorious Army of the Architect, though they never really got completely undressed. But that was with Denizens. Suzy, though he could forget about it most of the time, was practically a normal human girl. "Why do we have to take our clothes off?"

"The paint is transformative — it will prepare you to become a Raised Rat," Scamandros answered. "The activation I shall write upon the rind of the cheese, and then when you eat it, you will become a Raised Rat. I think."

"Okay," muttered Arthur. He turned back to look out the window and hesitantly undressed.

"Least there's ain't no bibliophages wanting to have a nibble on any writing, like," said Suzy. "You had writing all over your other clothes, Arthur. Is that what they do back home these days?"

"Yes," said Arthur. He took a deep breath and slipped off his underwear. "Start painting, Scamandros."

"He's painting me," said Suzy. "You'll 'ave to wait. Youch, that's cold paint!"

Arthur bit back an order to hurry up and focused on the view out the window. He didn't know what to do with his hands. Putting them on his hips seemed ridiculous when naked, but so did just letting them hang. Finally he folded them at the front, even though he thought that probably didn't look too good either.

"Right, Lord Arthur, here we go," said Scamandros. The next second Arthur felt a slap of cold fluid on his back, and flinched.

"Steady!" instructed Scamandros. "Haven't any to waste."

Arthur gritted his teeth and stood very still as Scamandros quickly brushed paint from his head to his heels.

"Very good, Lord Arthur. Turn around, if you please."

Arthur shut his eyes and slowly turned around. He heard a knock at the door at the same time, and a Raised Rat called out, "Got that cheese for you, sir. I'll just put it here."

"Arms up, Lord Arthur," said Scamandros cheerily.

Arthur screwed his eyes shut even tighter and quickly raised his arms. He couldn't help flinching as the paint went on some delicate areas.

"You're done!" said Scamandros.

Arthur opened his eyes and looked down. He'd been expecting to see gray paint on himself, but instead he saw a fine coat of gray-black fur that covered him from ankle to wrist like a hairy wet suit.

Though the fur went some way to preserving his modesty, Arthur quickly sat down, crossed his legs, and draped his coat across his lap.

"You won't have tails," said Scamandros sadly. "Couldn't do it. But quite a few of the Rats go without, having lost them in sea fights and the like."

He picked up the slab of cheese, broke it into two equal parts, and started writing with a peacock-feather pen he dipped in a tiny bottle of activated ink no larger than Arthur's little fingernail.

"I could get used to fur," said Suzy. "Saves washin' and changin' clothes."

Arthur raised his eyebrows.

"I do wash 'em," Suzy protested. "And change 'em. Lot of Denizen clothes clean themselves, you know. And change to fit. I wonder if this fur gets all manky in the rain. . . ."

"The cheese is ready," said Dr. Scamandros. He held up the two pieces, each roughly triangular and about ten inches long.

"Do we have to eat it all?" Arthur didn't sound excited by the prospect.

"Um, perhaps not." Scamandros hesitated. "About two-thirds should do the trick . . . but it would be best to err on the side of completion."

"Right," said Arthur. "All we need now is Lieutenant Finewhisker to open the Nebuchadnezzar — oh, I almost forgot. You were going to give me something to hide the Key's thingummies —"

Dr. Scamandros nodded and fossicked about inside his coat for a few moments before bringing out a crumpled piece of glittering metallic cloth that looked rather like a crushed tinfoil hat. He smoothed it out and pushed the edges apart, revealing that it was a small rectangular bag.

"Put the Key in there, and they won't sniff it out," he said, handing it over. "At least not unless they're very close and looking for it."

Arthur took the mirror-shaped Fifth Key and put it in the bag. He pulled its drawstring tight, then opened it again, to put Elephant inside as well. Then after almost closing it, he added the Mariner's medal that he'd been wearing on a makeshift dental-floss chain around his neck. With all three items safely in the bag, he finally drew the drawstring tight and tied the cord securely around his left wrist.

"The cheese will complete your transformation," said Scamandros.

"Except the Raised Rats usually wear clothes, so we'll need some too," said Arthur. "We should get some of the sailor's breeches or *something*. Is there anything in that chest over there?"

No one moved.

"Have a look, please, Suzy," Arthur said.

Finally Suzy wandered over, threw open the chest, and rummaged about, retrieving several very fine uniforms that must have belonged to Lieutenant Finewhisker. Suzy threw a pair of breeches and a white shirt over to Arthur, and put on a similar set herself. She looked longingly at a long, swallow-tailed coat with its swirling azure patterns before reluctantly returning it to the chest.

"Keep track of my gear, Doc," she said to Scamandros. "I'll be wanting it, by and by."

"I guess we're good to go," said Arthur. He looked across at Suzy and raised his cheese. She raised her lump back, as if making a toast.

"Let's eat!" said Arthur, and he bit his cheese.

It wasn't very tasty cheese. Arthur swallowed another huge mouthful and felt suddenly quite sick, the cabin spinning as it never had before. He started to say something about seasickness, and the change in the swell, but stopped. He was dizzy because he was shrinking and his eyes were moving in his head. His field of vision was changing — the things in front of him were harder to see, but he could see far more to the sides. The cabin was brighter than it had been too.

"Excellent!" exclaimed Scamandros. A tattooed torrent of Rats ran out from under his neckcloth and up the side of his face. "It works."

"Yes," said Arthur. He looked down at his odd, foreshortened arms and saw they ended in pink paws. "I'm a Raised Rat."

His voice was higher-pitched and husky. He raised one paw to check that the bag with the Key and Elephant was still there. It felt much heavier than it had before, but it was securely fastened.

Arthur slowly began to get dressed, his paws fumbling till he got used to them, and to his different vision. He'd just finished doing up his trouser buttons when Lieutenant Finewhisker knocked and entered the cabin without waiting for a reply. He saluted Arthur, who inclined his snout in greeting.

"Ready for the Nebuchadnezzar, Lord Arthur?" Finewhisker asked.

"Yes," Arthur replied.

"Very nice clothes you have on, if I may say so," said Finewhisker cheerily. "Excellent taste. Now, a twist here, a twist on the other side . . ."

He deftly removed the wire cage that held the cork in place, and then gently turned the huge cork, easing it out. It made a screeching fingernails-on-the-blackboard noise as it slowly revolved out, and then a surprisingly small *pop* as it came free and Finewhisker staggered back with it in his arms.

A thin waft of smoke billowed out the neck of the bottle — black, choking coal smoke.

"You need to jump straight through the neck,"

Finewhisker instructed. "A good strong jump with your paws forward. Avoid touching the glass if you can."

"Thank you, Finewhisker," said Arthur. "Thank you too, Doctor Scamandros. I will see you at the Citadel, I hope."

"Good luck, Lord Arthur," said the sorcerer. He bowed and added, "The spell will last a few hours, I should think."

"Come on, Arthur!" said Suzy. She hopped over to the bottle and tensed, ready to jump at the neck. "Last one in is a stinking ra . . . um . . . rabbit."

Arthur pulled her back by the scruff of her neck.

"Not this time, Suzy," he said. "I go first."

Suzy wriggled but didn't really resist as he moved her aside. Even as a Raised Rat, he was unnaturally strong, though it didn't occur to him that he shouldn't be able to pick up someone who weighed as much as he did, using only a paw.

With Suzy out of the way, Arthur took a few practice hops across the cabin. Then he stretched his paws and backed up to stand in the open cabin doorway, facing the open neck of the Simultaneous Nebuchadnezzar. Smoke was still wafting out of it, and the interior was dark and cloudy.

Bravery and stupidity can be quite closely related, Arthur thought. *I wonder what this is going to be. . . .*

He bent his legs, rushed forward, and dived straight at the open neck of the bottle.

He was in midair when a terrible last-minute thought slipped into his head:

What if the Raised Rats are lying? What if this bottle takes me somewhere entirely unexpected?

Chapter Nine

Arthur had expected to land inside the huge green glass bottle, at least for a few seconds before he was transferred, but instead he found himself diving *out* of the neck of a completely different Nebuchadnezzar, one made of sparkling blue glass. He landed heavily on a floor made of lozenge-patterned iron mesh, which hurt and left an imprint of itself on his fur.

Arthur rolled to a stop and immediately got up. He hardly had a moment to look around before a Raised Rat he only barely recognized as Suzy crashed into him and they both went sprawling on the iron floor again. They were disentangling themselves when a harsh, low voice spoke.

"Quickly now! Help me move the bottle! They'll be on to us in a minute or two."

Arthur jumped up and looked around. The blue Nebuchadnezzar was on a lashed-together wooden trolley with uneven wheels, and pushing it was the strangest, ugliest Piper's child that Arthur had ever seen. He wore a black cloak and a broad-brimmed hat with a feather, but even under the shadow of the brim, Arthur could see that the boy had a lumpy face and a ridiculously large nose.

The Nebuchadnezzar, Arthur, Suzy, and the ugly Piper's child were all on a broad metal walkway suspended from the ceiling by bronze rods every few yards. Though it was twelve feet wide, it had no rails, and was wreathed in smoke and steam.

Arthur gingerly peered over the edge. There was nothing beneath the walkway, no sign of solid ground. All he could see was a thick cloud of roiling black smoke. He could hear the whoosh, hiss, and deep bass beat of big steam engines somewhere down below, but he couldn't see any sign of them.

Then the smoke currents whorled and shifted and he caught a glimpse of the upper half of a huge bronze wheel as big as a house. It was turning very slowly, but before Arthur could see what it was connected to or what its purpose was, more smoke billowed across and obscured it again.

Closer to the walkway, a black cloud parted to reveal the end of a huge, rusted iron beam that was as long as three school buses joined together. The beam rose up through the smoke like a whale breaching, then descended into the depths with a gargling *whoosh,* and the industrial fog closed up again.

The metal mesh under Arthur's feet was vibrating in time to the beat of the engines below, and the bronze supporting rods hummed at Arthur's touch. The rods were tarnished, Arthur noted with concern, and their connection to the ceiling looked none too secure, though it was hard to see exactly how the thirty-foot-long rods were joined to the stone above. Judging by the occasional clean patches, the ceiling was a solid, pale rock, but most of it was so stained with soot that it resembled a dirty carpet of the blackest plush.

"Hurry! Help me push!" cried the Piper's child. He was struggling to get the bottle moving.

Arthur cautiously ran around the right-hand side of the bottle while Suzy ran around the left. They put their shoulders to the base of the Nebuchadnezzar and heaved. The trolley creaked and rumbled forward, slowly gathering speed. It had a tendency to veer dangerously off toward the edge, so all three pushers needed to be constantly vigilant.

"Got to get it back to the lubricant store," wheezed the Piper's child. "Fill it up with oil again and make ourselves scarce. You'll need disguises too."

Arthur glanced across at the boy and did a double take. It wasn't a Piper's child at all under the broad-brimmed hat with the scarlet feather, but a Raised Rat wearing a papier-mâché mask painted to look like a human face. The ridiculous nose covered the Rat's own snout.

"Lord Arthur, I presume," husked the Rat. "Dartbristle, at your service."

"Good to meet you," said Arthur. "This is my friend Suzy."

"General Suzy Turquoise Blue if you don't mind," sniffed Suzy.

"Welcome to the Upper House, General," said Dartbristle. "Up ahead, we need to heave her around to the left. Hurry now."

The walkway met another broader walkway at a T intersection. Manhandling the trolley around without it — or them — falling off the edge was no easy task, but they got it turned and were able to push the Nebuchadnezzar faster once they were in the clear.

Dartbristle kept looking behind them, so Arthur looked too, but all he could see was the thick, gray smoke, with occasional eddies of thicker, blacker smoke coiling up through it. He was no longer surprised that the smoke had no effect upon him. In fact, he even quite liked the smell, though he knew that his old human lungs would have quickly failed in the toxic atmosphere.

"What are you looking for?" Arthur asked after they had pushed the bottle several hundred feet and there was nothing to see ahead or behind except more of the platform and more of the smoke.

"Rat-catcher automatons," said Dartbristle. "The sorcerers know when the Nebuchadnezzar fires up — least they know there's serious sorcery afoot — but it takes 'em a minute or two to plot where it occurred. Since we're under the floor, they don't come down here themselves. They send Rat-catchers. But I reckon we might have gotten away fast enough. Lubricant store's just ahead, in the bulwark rock."

"We're under the floor of the Upper House?" asked Arthur.

"Yep." Dartbristle moved around to the front of the bottle and slowed it down as they came up to a sheer and apparently solid rock face of grimy yellow stone that was shot through with barely visible veins of a glowing purple metal. "We're in the bulwark between the Middle and the Upper House. Saturday had a bit of the top part of it burrowed out to put in all her steam engines, chain gear, and so on. Where is that bell push?"

The Rat began pressing different protuberances of rock, but none of them moved in the slightest.

"Curse the thing, always moving around. You'd think it was made by a practical joker!" Dartbristle griped.

"There's something behind us," said Suzy. "I saw something go under the walkway."

"Rat-catcher!" hissed Dartbristle. He reached under the Nebuchadnezzar and drew out three long curved knives from the trolley, handing one to Suzy and one to Arthur. "They're armored, so you need to get them in the red glowing bit right on the front of their head. I suppose it's an eye or something like it. But watch out for its nippers. And the feelers — they're like the tentacles of a Blackwater squid."

He spoke quickly and unhooked the mask off his face so it dangled under his mouth, allowing him to see better. His deep black eyes moved rapidly from side to side, and his nose twitched as he tried to smell the approaching enemy. Suddenly he started forward and raised his knife.

"Where is —" Suzy started to say, when all of a sudden the Rat-catcher automaton sprang out from under the walkway. Darting forward in a flash of steely plates and accompanied by a sound like the soft chink of coins in a leather purse, the twelve foot-long, two-foot-wide, metallic praying mantis opened its huge claws and nipped at Dartbristle. At the same time, its impossibly long, razor-edged feelers whipped at Arthur and Suzy.

Dartbristle ducked under and around one set of pincers

and heaved on the joint, pushing the automaton's left claw into its right, whereupon they gripped each other tightly. Suzy jumped back from a feeler. It cut her across the chest and tried to wrap itself around her neck to cut her head off, but she blocked it with her knife and slid under the Nebuchadnezzar trolley.

Arthur instinctively parried with his knife and twisted it to trap the feeler. Then, without thinking, he grabbed it and heaved. The razor edges cut his hand, which hurt, but he also managed to pull the feeler entirely out of the Rat-catcher's head, which caused a great fizz of sparks to jet out like a firework.

"Get the red eye!" shouted Dartbristle. "While the claws are locked!"

Arthur ran forward. The automaton's remaining feeler whipped at his legs, but he jumped over it, leaping so high that he landed on the Rat-catcher's back. The automaton immediately threw itself backwards, but he gripped it around its triangular head and plunged his knife deep into the red orb at the head's center. The little bag that held the Fifth Key knocked against the Rat-catcher's metal overlapping metal plates as Arthur stabbed the automaton several more times, before at last it gave a high-pitched, almost electronic squeal and slowly collapsed to the walkway, its rear legs hanging over the edge.

Arthur carefully climbed down, anxious not to over-balance the defunct automaton and send both of them down into the smoky depths. As soon as the boy stood safe on his own feet, Dartbristle began to push the Rat-catcher over the side.

"They can track these too," he said. "More come to find the remains, whenever one is slain."

Arthur helped him push, and Suzy slid out and gave the Rat-catcher a not very helpful but certainly satisfying kick just as it tumbled over.

"Right — I'll get that door open," said Dartbristle. He looked admiringly at Arthur and added, "Well fought, Lord Arthur."

"Thanks," said Arthur absently. He looked at his paw and saw that it was already almost healed, the gold blood disappearing as it dried. Belatedly he remembered that Suzy had been hurt.

"Suzy, that feeler cut you! Are you all right?"

Suzy, who had been looking over the side, turned around. Her shirt was cut through and gaped open, and there was a line of blood across her furry stomach, blood that was neither the blue of a Denizen nor entirely the red of a human, but something in between.

"Nah, I've had worse," Suzy said dismissively. "If I'd 'ad my old coat on, it would never have even broken the skin. Give it a day or two to scab up and I'll be right as rain."

"Found it!" declared Dartbristle. He pushed energetically on a slight knob of rock that was at the level of his knee. His push was answered by a rumble inside the stone. Slowly, a great rock-slab door as wide as the walkway pivoted open.

"In with the bottle," ordered Dartbristle. He started pushing the trolley, and Arthur quickly joined him. Suzy moved more slowly to help, and Arthur noticed she grimaced as she set her shoulder to the Nebuchadnezzar and began to push.

Beyond the door — which creaked shut behind them — was a rough-hewn stone chamber the size of a small auditorium, with a very high ceiling. Huge glass bottles as large or larger than the Simultaneous Nebuchadnezzar were lined up against the walls, and in front of them were stacked many smaller bottles, jars, jugs, urns, and other containers of glass, metal, or stoneware.

There was an open space on one wall between an amber bottle full of a dark viscous fluid and a nine-foot-tall clear glass bottle filled with what looked like light green olive oil. Dartbristle pointed at this gap and they maneuvered the Nebuchadnezzar to the space, untied it from the trolley, and began to lift it up.

"Hold it at an angle and lean it on that pot there," Dartbristle instructed. "Got to put some oil in it, so it doesn't look out of place. The purloined letter, you know."

"The what?" Arthur asked as Dartbristle picked up a Jeroboam-sized bottle and with great difficulty poured a stream of purple-black oil into the Nebuchadnezzar.

"Oh, yes, heard that one before," said Suzy. She left Arthur holding up the Simultaneous Bottle and wandered over to look at a small, narrow door on the other side of the chamber.

"Hide a letter by putting it in plain sight, where it will be considered ordinary," explained Dartbristle. "Good idea. Right, got to slap the cork in and then we'll be off."

"Off where exactly?" asked Arthur. "We need to get some clothes for when we stop being Raised Rats. This gear we have on won't fit."

"Exactly!" said Dartbristle. "Half a mo'."

He took off his hat, tipped it over, and took out a very small bottle, the kind that might hold perfume, and what Arthur at first thought was a cigarette pack. Dartbristle took a tiny rolled-up scroll out of the pack, checked what was written on the outside of it, unstoppered the bottle, and thrust the scroll in. He then replaced the stopper and put everything back into his hat, which he pulled firmly down upon his head, before also replacing his mask.

"Smallest Simultaneous Bottle there is," he said. He pointed to the Nebuchadnezzar. "One hundred and twentieth the size of that. Just had to report your arrival. Saturday's lot can't track the small bottle — it's sorcery on a scale too tiny for them to contemplate. Come on."

"I asked where we're going to," said Arthur frostily.

Really, these inferior creatures are galling. They should learn instant obedience —

Arthur shook his head and touched the bag at his wrist, feeling for Elephant.

I am not an angry, puffed-up superior Denizen, he thought sternly. *I am human. I am polite. I care about other people.*

"Up to the floor," said Dartbristle. "To join a Chain Gang. When you're back in normal shape you'll fit right in with the Piper's children. They're a good bunch; they'll take you on without too many questions. And they'll have clothes for you too."

"Very good," said Arthur. "How do we get there?"

"Service chain-haul. To shift the lubricants. We'll just grab hold and it'll take us up."

He took a small key from his hatband and trotted over to the narrow door. For the first time, Arthur noticed that, like himself, Dartbristle was a tail-less Raised Rat. But where Arthur didn't have a tail because Scamandros couldn't make one in time, Dartbristle had once had one, as evidenced by the battered stump of a tail poking out through an elegantly sewn hole in his black breeches.

The Raised Rat opened the door and pulled it open, revealing a vertical shaft about twelve feet square. In the middle of the shaft a heavy chain hung down. Each of its links was easily two feet tall and made from four-inch-thick dark iron. It wouldn't have been out of place on a battleship, Arthur thought.

"Got to start her up," said Dartbristle. He leaned precariously into the shaft and grabbed hold of the motionless chain, which was so heavy it barely rattled.

Arthur poked his head in and looked up and down. The chain extended in both directions as far as he could see into the smoke-shrouded shaft.

Dartbristle continued his instruction. "When she starts, you'd best jump and hold on quick, while she's still slow. Then wait for me to give the word to jump off, and jump. If you wait too long, the chain'll go over the wheel and take you back down again — or mash you up. Stand by the door . . . ready?"

Arthur and Suzy stood shoulder to shoulder in the doorway. Dartbristle shifted his grip, then swung fully onto the chain. As it took his weight, it fell a few feet, causing a frightful screech and rattle. Then there was a click almost as loud as a gunshot, and the chain began to move upward, taking Dartbristle with it.

Suzy jumped before Arthur could even think of doing so. She landed well, and climbed up a few feet to settle below Dartbristle's rear paws.

"I like this!" she exclaimed, and was gone, the chain already accelerating.

Arthur gulped, and leaped for the chain.

Chapter Ten

Arthur hit his snout on the chain, but got a good pawhold, gripping the link he held with remarkable strength. The chain was rising up at a speed that felt like forty or fifty miles an hour, the smoky air whistling past them fast enough to plaster Arthur's long Rat ears against his head.

"Uh-oh," said Suzy.

"What?" Arthur asked. He looked up. Suzy was only holding on with one paw while she wriggled her other paw in the air. "What are you doing?! Hold on with both hands . . . paws . . . whatever!"

"That's it!" said Suzy. "I can't. My paw is turning back into a hand and it's not working properly!"

"Hold on with your teeth!" called Dartbristle. He demonstrated with his own front teeth, which were at least five inches long and rather impressive.

"Can't!" said Suzy. "My mouth has gone weird and wobbly!"

She slithered down the chain toward Arthur. She looked half-Rat and half-human. He climbed up to her, and one human and one Raised Rat foot scraped his head before landing on his shoulders.

"Almost there!" called Dartbristle. "I'll count. Jump on three — it doesn't matter which direction."

"Can't . . . hold on!"

Suzy crashed into Arthur. He gripped the chain with his own huge front teeth and one paw and grabbed her with the other paw. He wasn't exactly sure what he was holding on to, because her body was rippling and changing, parts of it Raised Rat and parts human. It looked very disturbing and very painful, and her sailor's clothes were now nothing but rags, ripped and torn by the transformations.

"One!"

Suzy slipped from Arthur's grasp, but he swung his feet out and gripped her with his back paws, which in Rat shape were almost as dexterous as his front paws.

"Two!"

They shot out of the narrow shaft into a huge, dirty warehouse that was two-thirds full of the same kind of oil containers as the chamber below.

"Three! Jump!" shouted Dartbristle.

Arthur opened his mouth and pushed off from the chain, using all his strength so he took Suzy with him. The two of them landed on the edge of the shaft, and he had to scrabble and claw his way to safety, dragging Suzy with his back paws.

Above them, the chain continued up through a broad chimney to some other chamber, and Arthur caught a glimpse of the enormous, fast-spinning driving wheel that had pulled the chain.

"I'm going to kick Scamandros in the shins when I see him next!" growled Suzy. She stood up and then immediately fell down again as her lower half became human and her top half Raised Rat, so she was totally out of proportion and her center of gravity was all wrong.

"I'm sure it will wear off . . . ugh . . . soon," said Arthur. He had to pause mid-sentence as a wave of nausea ran through his body. His torso suddenly stretched up several feet, then snapped back again, and his paws turned to four sets of feet.

"It'd better," said Suzy. "Thanks, Arthur."

She crawled away from the shaft, and, after a moment's thought, Arthur followed her. The rapid changes to his body might topple him in if he stayed too close to the edge.

"I'll scout out the lay of the land while you're sorting yourselves out," said Dartbristle. "The grease monkeys — that's what the Piper's children here call themselves — have a depot across the way, and there's a drain that connects us here. We can't cross outside, because there's a detachment of Sorcerous Supernumeraries watching the depot, but I'll nip through, have a word with the grease monkeys, and pick you up some clothes."

"Don't tell them our real names," said Arthur. He had an unbearably itchy nose, but he couldn't control his arms enough to be able to scratch it. "Tell them . . . uh . . . tell them we're Piper's children discharged from the Army and we've just been washed between the ears and can't remember our names or anything yet."

"Aye, aye," said Dartbristle. He went over to a nearby trapdoor and lifted it. As he did, the sound of rushing water — a great deal of rushing water — filled the warehouse.

"Got to wait a few minutes," he said. "This is a flood channel — takes an overflow every now and again. Timing is everything, as they say."

"Quiet!" Arthur suddenly ordered. He sat up as best he could with a rubbery neck and cocked his one Rat ear to listen. Amid the sound of the rushing water, he'd heard a distinctive call, and at the same time he'd felt a familiar twinge inside his head.

"Arthur!"

It was the Will, calling his name. But the voice was distant and fleeting. Even with the others quiet, all he could hear now was running water, the jangle of the moving chain in the shaft, and the more distant thrum of the subterranean engines.

"Did you hear that?" he asked. "Someone calling my name?"

"No," said Suzy. She looked herself again. Even the torn rags of her Rat breeches and shirt weren't that out of place on her, considering her normal choice in clothes. "Didn't hear nuthin'."

"Nor I, I fear," added Dartbristle. "And with my ears, I have won many a Hearing Contest in the fleet."

"Never mind," said Arthur.

It must have been speaking in my head, he thought. *Like the Carp did . . . but from far away. Or perhaps the Will could only escape its bonds for a moment. . . .*

The sound of the rushing water died away. Dartbristle waved his hat over his head and jumped down. Arthur and Suzy could hear the splash as he landed in the channel.

"There's a window up there," said Suzy, pointing to a large iron-barred window of dirty, rain-flecked glass that was set into the riveted iron walls about twelve feet up. "If I climb up those bottles, and stand on top of that big yellow one, I reckon I could see outside."

The window let in a subdued grayish light. Looking at it, Arthur realized for the first time that he must have developed better night vision, because he could see quite clearly, even though the warehouse had only one dim lantern hanging from the high ceiling, and the six windows, all on the same wall, did not admit much extra light.

"Suzy, how light is it in here?" he asked.

"In here? If it weren't for the windows and that lantern, it'd be dark as a dog's dinner, inside of a dog, and even with the windows and the lantern it's not much better," answered Suzy, who was starting to climb from one bottleneck to another, stepping across an impromptu stairway to her chosen window. "But I reckon it is daytime outside, only it's raining."

"What can you see?" Arthur was now almost himself, apart from his hands, which were still paws and not under his control. They were twitching and wriggling in a very annoying way and he had already slapped himself in the face several times and would have suffered more if he hadn't gotten control of his arms and neck and twisted away. His clothes were also reduced to shreds, which was probably just as well, as they would have been terribly restrictive now that he was back to his full height.

"Rain," said Suzy. "And not much else. There's a very tall building, with lots of green lights."

"Ow!" said Arthur as his paws turned into hands but

kept twitching, smacking his fingers against the floor. "That's enough! Stop!"

His hands tingled and stopped. Arthur flexed his fingers and gave a relieved sigh. He was himself again, and everything was under control.

Suzy climbed down and both of them went over to look through the trapdoor. There was a rusted iron ladder that led down to an arched passage lined with small red bricks. A thin trickle of water ran down the middle, but from the dampness of the walls it was evident that the water rose nearly as high as the trapdoor when it was in full spate, as it must have been just a few minutes before the Raised Rat went through.

Suzy immediately started to climb down the ladder, but Arthur pulled her back.

"Hold on! Let's wait for Dartbristle. We need proper clothes. Besides, there might be more water flooding through."

"I was just 'aving a look," grumbled Suzy.

"How's that cut?" asked Arthur.

Suzy looked down and felt her chest through her ripped rags.

"It's gone!" she exclaimed. "That was at least a four-day cut, that was!"

"Healed in the transformation, I suppose," said Arthur.

"Maybe I won't kick old Doc after all," said Suzy cheerfully.

"I'm glad you're better." Arthur knelt down and peered into the flood channel. Though it wasn't lit at all, he could see at least thirty or forty feet along it. That made him have a second thought about his eyes, and he sprang back up and looked carefully at Suzy. Her eyes looked the same as ever: dark brown, curious, and sharp.

"Suzy," he said. "My eyes haven't stayed like a Raised Rat's, have they?"

"Nope. They've gone bright blue, but. Wot's called cornflower blue in the inkworks. Only yours is kind of glowing. I reckon it's to do with the Keys turning you into . . . whatever it is they're turning you into."

"A Denizen," said Arthur glumly.

"Nah," said Suzy. "Not even a Superior Denizen looks like you do. When that Dartbristle gets back, we'd best smear some grease on your face so you'll pass as one of us."

I can't even be mistaken for a Piper's child anymore, thought Arthur with unexpected sadness.

Suzy cocked her head, sensing his mood.

"You'll still be Arthur Penhaligon," she said. "Not the brightest, not the bravest, but up for anything. Least, that's how I see you. Kind of like a little brother, only you're taller than me now."

She paused and frowned. "I think I had a little brother once. Don't know whether it was here, or back home, or what . . ."

She stopped talking, and their eyes met briefly. They both remembered the Improbable Stair and their visit to Suzy's original home, back on Earth, back in time, a city in the grip of the bubonic plague. If Suzy had once had a brother, he'd likely died young and long ago, stricken by the disease.

That reminded Arthur of the plagues back home, the modern ones, and the hospital, and the Skinless Boy who had taken his place, and his brother calling about the nuclear strike on East Area Hospital. He felt a tide of anxiety rise up from somewhere in his stomach, almost choking him with responsibilities. He had to find the Will here, and defeat Saturday, and get back home in time to do something about the nuclear attack before it happened. . . .

"It's not a good idea to stop breathing," said Suzy, interrupting Arthur's panic attack. She clapped him on the back and he took a sudden intake of breath.

"I know," he said. "It's just, it's just —"

"Ahoy there, children!"

Dartbristle climbed out of the flood channel, carrying a large cloth bag marked LAUNDRY. He tipped it up and emptied a pile of clothes and boots onto the floor.

"Help yourself," he said. "Stuff should resize to fit, if it ain't worn out. I picked up a few sets to be sure."

The clothes were dirty off-white coveralls that had lots of pockets. Arthur picked up a set, hesitated a moment, then stripped off his rags and put on the coveralls as quickly as he could. The coveralls immediately resized themselves to fit, and several oil stains moved around as well to get better positions, some bickering before they established their preeminence.

"Odd clothes," said Suzy doubtfully. She put on the coveralls, but tore a strip of blue cloth off her old rags and added it as a belt.

"You'll get utility belts at the depot," said Dartbristle.

"I like a bit of color," sniffed Suzy.

"There's boots there," Dartbristle pointed out. "You'll need them for the climbing and jumping and whatnot."

"Climbing and jumping?" asked Arthur. He sat down and pulled on a pair of the boots. They were made of soft leather and had strange soles that were covered in tiny tentacles like a sea anemone. They gripped Arthur's finger when he touched them.

"Everything up past the ground-floor level here is made up of desk units," said Dartbristle. "Open iron boxes with a lattice floor, stacked and slotted into a framework of guide rails, and moved up, down, and across by shifter chains. The Piper's children here are grease monkeys — they keep the chains oiled, free up obstructions, service the pneumatic message tubes, and so on. Requires a lot of climbing, jumping, and the like. If you're going to be looking around the Upper House, you'll need to fit in as grease monkeys."

"Who said we'd be looking around the Upper House?" asked Arthur suspiciously.

Perhaps I should slay this Rat now, came an unbidden thought. *He knows too much and I probably don't need him. . . . Stop . . . stop! I don't want these thoughts. . . .*

"The message that came through advising me of your arrival," Dartbristle replied. "Said you'd be looking for something, and to offer you any reasonable assistance."

"Yes," said Arthur, keeping a tight lid on the nasty, selfish thoughts that were roiling about in the depths of his head. "Thank you. We are looking for something. In fact —"

He took a breath and decided to go for it. He had to trust people, even if they happened to be Raised Rats. Or Denizens. Or Piper's children.

"I'm looking for Part Six of the Will of the Architect. It's here somewhere. Trapped, or held prisoner. Have you heard anything about it?"

Dartbristle took off his hat and scratched his head. Then he took off his mask and scratched his nose. Then he put both back on and said, "No, I'm afraid not. The grease monkeys might —"

"Maybe," said Arthur. "But I want to check them out first, so keep it secret for now. Remember, we're newly returned from the Army and washed between the ears."

"Aye, I'll remember," said Dartbristle. "We're good with secrets, we Raised Rats. Are you ready to go?"

The question was addressed to Suzy, who was playing with the sole of one of her boots.

"Reckon," she said, slipping on her footwear. "Down that tunnel?"

"Yes, we have to avoid the Sorcerous Supernumeraries, as I said," replied Dartbristle. "We should have an hour or more before the next flood."

"How can you tell?" Arthur asked. He looked up at the window. "Doesn't it depend on the rain?"

"Yes and no," said Dartbristle as he led the way down

the ladder. "You see, it always rains here, and always at the same, steady rate. Makes traversing the flood channels and stormwater drains very predictable."

"It always rains?" asked Arthur. "Why?"

"She likes the rain," Dartbristle told him. "Or maybe she likes umbrellas."

There was no doubt who "she" was: Superior Saturday, who Arthur was beginning to think more and more must be his ultimate nemesis, and the cause of not only his own troubles but those of the entire House and the Universe beyond.

Now he was in her demesne. She, and her thousands of sorcerers, were somewhere up above him. Hopefully in ignorance of his presence, but possibly all too aware that he had come within her reach.

Chapter Eleven

As Dartbristle had claimed, the flood channel did not suddenly fill with rushing water as Arthur half-feared it might. All the way along he listened carefully for the sound of an approaching deluge, and was ready to race back to the ladder and the warehouse. Then, when he caught sight of a ladder ahead, he had to hold himself back from trampling over the Raised Rat to get to it and climb out.

Maybe all my worries have made me claustrophobic, Arthur thought with some concern. But then he told himself it was perfectly normal to be concerned when walking along what was basically a big underground drain, in the middle of a heavy rainstorm. People got drowned all the time doing stupid stuff like that, and as he had thought before in the Border Sea, Arthur was particularly concerned that the Key would keep him sort of alive underwater and he might take a long time to die.

However, he managed to stay calm, and didn't streak up the ladder like a rat up a drainpipe. Instead he remembered what Suzy had said about his looks, and paused to pick up some mud, which he smeared on his face and front.

After that he climbed out slowly, and so had time to adjust to the light and noise that was filtering down the access shaft to the channel.

The chamber above was very different from the warehouse. It was smaller, sixty feet square, and had thick stone walls without any windows and only a single door, which was shut and barred. But it was full of light, from the dozens of lanterns that hung from wires of different lengths from the arch-beamed ceiling high above, and it was full of noise, from the thirty or so grease monkeys who were sitting on simple wooden benches at six old oak tables — or not sitting, since a good number of them were jumping over the tables as part of a dozen-person game of tag, or doing cartwheels along them, or playing shuttlecock with improvised shuttles and bats, or constructing curious pieces of machinery. Or completely monopolizing a tabletop by lying asleep on it, as one nearby grease monkey was doing.

As Dartbristle helped Suzy out and she and Arthur stood at the rim of the trapdoor, all this activity ceased. The children stopped their games and activities and turned to look at the new arrivals.

"Wotcher!" said Suzy, and went to tip her hat. She got halfway to her head before she remembered it wasn't there, and so had to be satisfied with a wave.

The grease monkeys didn't wave back. They stood there, staring, until the one who was apparently asleep on the table rubbed her eyes and sat up. She looked like a typical Piper's child, with her ragged, self-cut hair, dirty face, and oil-stained coveralls. But from the way the other grease monkeys' eyes shifted toward her, Arthur could tell she was the boss.

"Mornin'," she said. "Dartie here says you've been demobbed and sent back, with a washing between the ears behind you."

"That's right," said Arthur. "Uh, I think."

"I'm Alyse Shifter First Class," said the girl. "I'm gang boss of this bunch, the Twenty-seventh Chain and Motivation Maintenance Brigade of the Upper House. What're your names and classifications? Don't tell me your House precedence — we don't bother with that here."

"Uh ... I can't quite ... remember," said Arthur. "I think my name's Ray."

"Got your paperwork?" asked Alyse, holding out her hand.

"Lost it," muttered Arthur.

"Somewhere," added Suzy vaguely. "Think my name's Suze, though."

"Suze and Ray," said Alyse. "Well, what's your classification?"

"Uh . . ." Arthur let his voice trail off as he looked around in what he hoped was a gormless manner, till he spotted a long line of coats and other items hanging from coat hooks down the far wall. Each hook held a duckling-yellow peaked rain-cap, a rubberized yellow rain-mantle, and a broad leather belt loaded with pouches, tools, and a holster that held a long, shining silver shifting wrench.

"I think I used to do up nuts," he said. "For bolts?"

Alyse looked at him.

"You got long enough arms for it," she said. "Nut-turner, I guess. Maybe First Class. What about you?"

"Dunno," said Suzy. "Forget. Reckon I could turn my hand to anything, though."

Alyse looked her up and down and shrugged.

"Nice under-belt," she said. "Blue-sky wisher, are you? You must be a Wire-flyer?"

"Maybe," agreed Suzy guardedly.

"What's a Wire-flyer?" Arthur asked.

"You *did* get scrubbed good and proper," said Alyse. "Try and remember! I'm talking installation, not main-tenance. A Wire-flyer flies the guide wires up, so as the Rail-risers can put up the rails for the Chain-runners and the Hook-'em-ups can slot in the desk unit and the Nut-holders and Bolt-turners make it fast and the Shifter gives the word. Only if we're not building up, the Wire-fliers do odd jobs, help out the Chain-oilers, stuff like that. Coming back to you now?"

"A . . . a bit," said Arthur. He didn't need to act confused by her explanation.

"Have to see it, I reckon," said Suzy. "Picture paints a thousand words. Is that tea over there?"

"It'll come back to you," declared Alyse, ignoring Suzy's question. She held out her palm, spat in it, and offered her hand to Arthur. "Welcome to the Twenty-seventh Chain and Motivation Maintenance Brigade, or as we like to call it —"

"Alyse's Apes!" roared the assembled grease monkeys.

Arthur shook hands, and Alyse spat again. Suzy spat on her own hand and Arthur thought he should have spat on his too, and hoped his recently washed-between-the-ears state would let him be forgiven for this lapse in Piper's child etiquette.

"Tea's in the pot," said Alyse, pointing to the huge teapot that was simmering on a trivet above a glass spirit burner in the corner. She then pointed to a large and decrepit-looking cuckoo clock that had half-fallen off the wall and was slumped just above the floor at an odd angle. Its hands still moved and Arthur could hear the quiet *thock-thock-thock* of its inner workings. It said the time was seventeen minutes to twelve.

"Help yourself. Shift starts at twelve, so get a cup down you while you can. Don't forget to check your gear before noon."

Alyse yawned and began to lie back down on the table-top, but one of the other grease monkeys called out, "Alyse! Which pegs do they get?"

Alyse scowled and sat back up again.

"Never a moment's rest," she sighed, though Arthur was sure she had been sound asleep when he arrived. She opened one of the pockets on her coverall and drew out a thick and well-thumbed notebook. "Let's see. Yonik was the last one to fall, so his peg's free — that's number thirty-three. Before that was Dotty —"

"But Dotty didn't fall; she just got her leg crushed," said one of the grease monkeys. "She'll be back."

"Not for three months or more," said Alyse. "So her peg and her belt are free. Them's the rules.

"Number twenty," she added to Suzy, pointing half-way along the line of coat hooks. "You're lucky — Dotty kept her gear very nice. Better than Yonik, which goes to show. He wouldn't have fallen if he'd kept his wings clean."

"And his nose," added someone, to general laughter.

"Was he badly hurt?" asked Arthur.

"Hurt?" Alyse laughed. "When you're working on the

tower, as we was, if you fall off and your wings don't work, you don't get hurt. You get dead. Even a Denizen can't survive that fall. Twelve thousand feet, straight down. We were lucky to find his belt and tools, and his wrench had to be replaced. Bent like a crescent, it was."

Arthur shook his head. He'd always thought Suzy was quite callous, but these Piper's children were even worse.

I suppose when you've lived a very, very long time, you feel differently about dying, he figured. *I wonder if I will feel the same . . . not that I'm likely to live that long. . . .*

A tug at his elbow interrupted his thoughts.

"I have to go," said Dartbristle. "Got work to do, and there's a flood due through right after twelve."

"Thank you," said Arthur. "I really appreciate your help."

He offered his hand, and bent down close to shake the Raised Rat's paw and whisper in his ear, "If you hear anything about Part Six of the Will, send word to me."

"Aye," said Dartbristle. "Good-bye, Ray and Suze."

"Thanks, Dart," said Suzy with a wave.

Once the Raised Rat was gone, she added, "Come and get yer tea, Ray," as she searched out two good-sized mugs from the dozens of chipped and damaged porcelain teacups and mugs that lay in disorganized piles around the spirit burner. Several grease monkeys who were gathered there to drink tea started to say hello, and Suzy poured tea with one hand as she spat and shook with the other.

"I'm going to check my stuff," Arthur called out, which was probably the wrong thing to do. The other grease monkeys went back to their activities, and none came to introduce themselves as he went over to his peg.

Arthur put on his rain-mantle, which was like a sleeveless raincoat with a hood that went over his peaked cap. The cap had a buckle to fasten under the chin. Beneath the cap on the peg was a pair of clear goggles, which Arthur tried on and adjusted to fit. In the single large pocket of the rain-mantle there was a folded pair of dirty yellow wings. Arthur took them out, shook them so they expanded to full size, and spent ten minutes plucking out pieces of grit and dirt before folding them back up again.

The utility belt was very heavy. One of the six pouches held several different sizes of nuts and bolts. Another had a moldy apple core in it, which Arthur removed. The next had a small grease gun, which was leaking until Arthur tightened the nozzle. The fourth pocket contained a pair of light leather fingerless gloves, which he put on. The fifth had an apparently unused cleaning cloth, small cleaning brush, and a cake of soap that had BEST QUALITY WATERLESS PERPETUAL SOAP stamped on it.

The sixth pouch was empty. Arthur tested its strap, then quickly slipped his elephant and the Fifth Key inside.

He looked around to see if anyone had seen him, but it looked like he had managed to be surreptitious. That done, he took the soap back out of the fifth pouch and tried it on an oily patch on his coveralls. Part of the stain was erased with surprising ease. Arthur was about to clean it off completely, but paused to look once more at the other grease monkeys, most of whom were now putting on their gear.

All of them had stained coveralls, and Alyse's coveralls were the most splotched of all, with at least a dozen different-colored oil stains.

Arthur quietly put the soap back in its pouch and put the belt on. Suzy was putting her belt on too, farther down the line. She waved at him and smiled.

Having fun as usual, thought Arthur. *She lives in the moment. I wish I could.*

He smiled a slight smile and waved back, then drew out his shifting wrench and hefted it, slapping the head against his palm. It was very shiny and *very* heavy. The screw-wheel that opened and shut the mouth of the wrench was gritted up, so Arthur quickly cleaned it with the brush and applied a spot of grease from his grease gun, not noticing that Alyse was watching him with approval.

"They can scrub us between the ears," she said, "but good workers never forget to look after their gear."

She climbed up onto one of the tables and waited expectantly. The last of the grease monkeys finished putting on his belt, and they all turned around to face their leader. Arthur and Suzy followed a beat behind.

"Are we ready?" asked Alyse.

"Ready!" called the grease monkeys.

"Then let's go!" Alyse jumped off the table and took her place at the head of the line. The grease monkeys did a right turn that would have made Arthur's old drill instructor Sergeant Helve start screaming at the informality and slovenliness of it. Completely out of step, they marched to the door.

Chapter Twelve

Alyse unbarred and opened the door. Splashing through the first puddle outside, she led the the grease monkeys out onto a rainy, cobble-paved square that was surrounded on three sides by warehouse-style buildings made of riveted iron, and on the fourth side by the sharp corner of a truly vast and massive construction.

There was a bedraggled reception committee waiting outside. A group of a dozen Denizens huddled under black umbrellas, wearing long black coats over gray waistcoats and pale blue shirts, with gray cravats and hats that were like top hats only not so tall. Their white trousers were tucked into green waterproof Wellington boots and they stood in a semicircular line around the door.

Alyse ignored them, splashing between them toward the huge building that Arthur figured was the one Suzy had spotted from the window of the warehouse. Now that they were closer, he could see it was a tower that stretched up and out of sight, its great bulk appearing to rise even higher than the pallid, rain-obscured sun that hung off to one side.

Arthur could now also see what he had been told — that this tower was completely made up of boxlike office units that had no walls and latticed floors, so you could see a long way up the inside. It was rather like looking into a modern glass skyscraper at night, if that skyscraper also had interior glass walls.

Judging from the closer offices, which Arthur could see into very distinctly, each one of these little boxes was inhabited by a Denizen working at a desk. Each desk had a green-shaded lamp and an umbrella over it. The umbrellas, Arthur noted, were of many different shades and colors, although he couldn't figure out why.

Arthur was second last in the line of grease monkeys. The grease monkey behind him stopped to shut the door behind them, then ran to catch up. He was a good foot shorter than Arthur, had brown hair as badly cut as Alyse's, and big sticking-out ears. Instead of marching behind Arthur, he walked next to him, spat on his palm, and offered his hand.

"Whrod," he said. "Bolt-turner Second Class. We'll probably be working together."

"Rod?" asked Arthur, remembering to spit this time before he shook.

"Whah-rod," said Whrod.

"Good to meet you," Arthur replied, but he was already

looking over Whrod's shoulder at the black-suited umbrella wielders who had begun to follow them in a doleful fashion.

"Don't mind them," said Whrod, following Arthur's glance. "Sorcerous Supernumeraries. Detailed to kill us if the Piper shows up and tries to make us do something. Terrible job for them, standing outside in the rain all night, not to mention trying to follow us all day and never quite managing to catch up. Still, they're used to disappointment."

"Uh, why?" Arthur asked. They certainly *looked* miserable. He'd never seen such mournful-looking Denizens. Even Monday's Midnight Visitors hadn't looked so terminally depressed.

"They're Sorcerous Supernumeraries, of course," said Whrod. "Failed their exams to become proper sorcerers and can't get a decent post in the Upper House. They've got no chance of moving up higher than the floor. . . . It gets them down."

"Why don't they leave? Go to some other part of the House?"

Whrod looked at Arthur.

"You did get a good washing, didn't you? No one leaves Superior Saturday's service. Unless you get drafted like you did, and then it's only for a hundred years. Besides,

I reckon they secretly enjoy being miserable. Gives them a focus in life. Come on, we're lagging behind."

Whrod walked faster, and Arthur picked up his pace. Behind them, the Sorcerous Supernumeraries followed at a gloomy lope.

Alyse led them into the base of the tower. Arthur thought they would go through a door and a corridor, but instead they just walked into an office, filing past the desk of a Denizen who was watching something in what looked like a shaving mirror. At the same time he was writing on two separate pieces of paper with a quill pen in each hand, occasionally dipping them in a tarnished copper-gilt inkwell. The umbrella that shielded his desk from the rain and the constant rush of water from above was dark brown and rather moldy, letting in numerous drips that somehow only fell on the Denizen and not on his work.

He didn't look up as the grease monkeys and their shadowing Sorcerous Supernumeraries filed past. Nor did the next one, or the next, or the one after that. By the fiftieth office, Arthur didn't expect one to do anything but look at their mirror and write feverishly.

At the fifty-first office, Alyse held up her hand and everyone halted. She climbed up to one corner of the Denizen's desk and, stretching to her full height, made some adjustment to a six-inch-wide pipe. Now that Arthur's attention was drawn to it, he saw that there was a network of similar pipes that ran through every office and horizontally under the floor of the offices above, with junctions every now and then for vertical pipes that ran up the corners of certain offices, like the one Alyse was in.

"What are those pipes?" Arthur asked Whron.

The grease monkey gave Arthur another look of disbelief.

"They done a job on you," he said. "Practically the village idiot. Those pipes —"

He was cut off as Arthur gripped him by the collar of his coveralls and lifted him up, twisting the cloth tight upon his throat.

"What did you call me?" he hissed.

"Arghh," Whron choked out. His right hand felt for the wrench at his side, but before he could draw it, Arthur grabbed his wrist with his left hand and squeezed.

"Ar — I mean, Ray — drop him!"

Suzy's voice penetrated the total focus of rage that had gripped Arthur. He shivered and let go, and Whron fell at his feet. Suzy ran up and slid to a halt next to him, immediately holding on to his arm. Arthur wasn't sure if it was a gesture of friendship and solidarity or a preparation to restrain him.

The Sorcerous Supernumeraries, who were spread out

through several adjoining offices, glided closer, some of them even forgetting themselves so much as to look directly at what was going on, rather than stare at the ground and take occasional furtive glances when required.

"Sorry," Arthur whispered. He lifted his head and took a gulp of air and a facefull of water, most of which splashed off his goggles. "Sorry . . . I think . . . my head's not quite right. I take insults badly."

Whron felt his throat, then got up.

"Didn't mean nothing by it," he said gruffly. "You're strong — stronger than anyone I ever met."

"A hundred years in the Army will do that," said Suzy. "Come along, Ray."

"What's the holdup?" called out Alyse from up front.

"Nothing! All sorted!" answered Suzy.

"I really am sorry," said Arthur. He offered his hand to Whron, who hesitated, then shook briefly. Neither of them spat, and Arthur wondered whether this meant anything. He couldn't tell under the peaked cap and the goggles whether Whron was looking at him with newly kindled hatred, curiosity, or some other emotion.

I'll have to watch my back. It's easy enough to fall if you're pushed, and even I might not survive a twelve-thousand-foot fall.

"The pipes," Whron said carefully, "are pneumatic

message tubes. For sending records and messages around. They're not used much down here, not among the lowest of the low. These clerks just copy stuff, and their papers are taken and delivered by slow messenger."

"Thanks," Arthur muttered.

They started walking again, trailing through more offices, mostly in a straight line with an occasional detour, such as one made to avoid an office that was essentially in the midst of a raging waterfall. The sodden Denizen there bravely continued to work on her completely dry papers as water cascaded from her head and shoulders, her stoved-in umbrella at her side.

Around the hundredth office, Arthur noticed a noise coming from somewhere ahead — a deep, rumbling noise that sounded as if there were a very large coffee grinder working away. It got louder as they continued walking, until it was so loud that it drowned out the sound of the rain, the drips, and even the *swoosh* of an occasional cascade from above.

The noise came from an open space up ahead, which Arthur could only glimpse through the offices, umbrellas, and the grease monkeys ahead of him.

When they got closer, he saw there was a small cleared area the size of several office units, bordered by massive vertical iron beams in each corner, with similar horizontal beams above at the next level of offices, and more beyond that, a square strut of iron box-work that went up and up and up.

In the middle of this shaft, two chains hummed and groaned and rattled. One went up and one went down, through a grilled hole that every few seconds emitted a waft of steam and smoke.

The chains were not like the one Arthur and Suzy had ridden up from the oil warehouse. They were more like bicycle chains, huge bicycle chains, with each link six feet wide and six feet high. In the space in the middle of each link, there were rings welded to the inside wall. Sometimes there were frayed ropes tied to these rings, and sometimes even a welded iron chair or a bench.

Both chains moved at the same rate — about as fast as Arthur could run, he gauged. As soon as he saw them, he knew that this was how the grease monkeys were going to get higher up in the tower.

Alyse stopped and gestured, and the line of grease monkeys spread out to gather around her.

"You know the drill," she said. "But we've got two washed-between-the-ears folk with us today, so we'll go over it again. This is the northeast Big Chain, which provides the main motivation power for all the northeast Little Chains. Because it's the Big Chain, we can travel two per link. We get on together, and we leave together. If you see the link looks oily or has a problem, you shout 'Wait' before your partner gets aboard it, and you take the next. Now, let's see —"

She took a piece of paper out of a pocket and unfolded it, at the same time hopping to the right to avoid a sudden downsplash.

"We're helping the automatons do a move today. There's someone going up from Level 6995 to Level 61012, and across forty-two offices on the diagonal chain. We'll do the vertical first and make it as quick as we can — we don't want to give this lucky chap's neighbors time to cause trouble. So we get off at 6995. Everyone got that? Suze and Ray?"

"Yes," said Arthur. Suzy nodded.

"Good," said Alyse. "Ray, come over here. You'll jump on the first link with me, and Suze, you jump on the second with Vithan."

Arthur splashed over to Alyse's side. She held out her hand commandingly and took his, almost dragging him toward the rising chain before he caught up.

"The trick is not to jump, because you'll probably fall," Alyse cautioned. "You just sidle up close and then step onto the rising link as it comes up."

"Whatever you say," said Arthur.

It wouldn't be so bad if only the chain wasn't going so fast, he thought. *I could get my leg torn off here. . . .*

"Come right up to it," Alyse instructed. They walked closer to the chain, moving around so they faced the open link and were only a step away. Arthur could feel the rush of the chain's movement, too close for comfort if a link swayed out of line. It still looked to be going too fast to simply step on.

"You ready?" asked Alyse.

"Yes," said Arthur, and he was — until a huge shower of water landed on top of him, so much water that the peak of his cap collapsed into his face and he leaned back and almost went down on one knee. In the middle of it all, he heard Part Six of the Will.

Arthur! You have to come and get me in the —

With a jerk, Alyse pulled him forward. Blinded by his collapsed cap and all the water in his eyes, Arthur had no choice but to step out, not knowing whether he was with her or had fallen that deadly half a step behind that would mean he would miss the inside of the link and instead fall into the grate and be mashed to bits by the next massive piece of the monster chain.

He stretched out and his foot went down. . . .

Chapter Thirteen

Leaf's eyes narrowed and she blinked hard several times. Arthur had vanished. One second he was there, and then he wasn't.

She looked around and scowled. Not only had Arthur disappeared but everyone else had become frozen —

The army is going to fire nukes at somewhere very close by, Leaf suddenly remembered. *At one minute past midnight. So why I am standing here with my mouth open like some stupid goldfish?*

"Arthur!" she shouted again. Then she started running, out through the ward with its frozen statues of sleepers. "Arthur!"

No one answered her. Leaf stopped at the end of the ward and looked around. Not only was everyone frozen, but there was also a kind of weird red light around them. Like a faint aura that she could only see when she looked out of the corner of her eyes. That same red glow was around the ward clock, high on the wall, which was stuck at three minutes to twelve.

Or not stuck. As Leaf looked, the red haze vanished.

The minute hand sprang forward, and simultaneously the ward came alive with shuffling sleepers. Leaf heard someone call out from the office. Not Arthur — a woman's voice. Probably Vess or Martine.

Two minutes! thought Leaf in panic. *There's not enough time to do anything. We're all going to die!*

The clock stopped. The sleepers became petrified once more. The red aura effect came back.

But Leaf could still hear the woman's voice, and it got louder and louder until Martine burst into the ward.

"What is going on? Where's Lord Arthur?"

"I don't know," Leaf said. "Is there anything underneath this hospital? I mean underground levels . . . even a bomb shelter?"

"I haven't been here for twenty years!" exclaimed Martine. "Ask Vess."

Leaf looked around, then pointed. Vess was standing frozen in a corner of the ward.

"Oh," Martine said. "Well, twenty years ago there were operating theaters on B3, and there was a bomb shelter once. I mean, this place was built in the fifties, so what do you expect?"

"We have to get everyone down there," said Leaf firmly. "You and me. As quickly as we can."

"But they're like statues. . . ."

"We'll wheel them in beds. Two or three to a bed. I wonder if the elevators work? The lights do." Leaf saw the hesitation on Martine's face. "Come on — help me load these two into this bed."

"I don't understand," Martine said. "I thought that once I finally got back home, everything would be all right. But I still don't understand anything. Why are we taking everyone downstairs? Why do we need a bomb shelter?"

"Arthur said the army is going to nuke East Area Hospital at 12:01 because it's a plague nexus. And East Area is not so far from here. Arthur's done something to stop time, I guess, but it restarted a moment ago. It could restart again in a second, or a minute, who knows! Please, we have to get going!"

"No," said Martine. "No."

She turned and ran away sobbing, crashing through the swing doors and disappearing.

Leaf stared after her for a microsecond, then went and examined the closest hospital bed. It had wheels with brakes on them, which she clicked off. There was already a sleeper in the bed, so she grabbed hold of the rail and pulled the bed out and swung it around. It was harder than she'd expected, possibly because the bed had not been moved in a long time.

"You're number one," she said to the man asleep in the bed. "We'll pick up Aunt Mango on the way, and that'll be two. After you, I'll only have approximately one thousand nine hundred and ninety-eight people to get to safety. In two and a half minutes."

It took Leaf a lot longer than two minutes to find the elevators, and then she was dismayed to find that they weren't working. Clearly, things that stayed the same from one moment to the next — like lightbulbs — continued to work while things that moved were stuck in place. Luckily, there was a map next to the elevator bank that showed where there was a wheelchair ramp to get to the lower floors.

She'd loaded not only her aunt Mango but two other people onto the bed. They were the two smallest she could find in the immediate vicinity of her aunt, but even so, her back ached from dragging them across the floor and then levering them onto the bed. They actually were like statues to move, though fortunately ones made of flesh and blood, not marble. Still, their rigidity made them difficult to shift and maneuver.

There was another wall map near the top of the ramp, but it didn't indicate where the operating theaters used to be, or the old bomb shelter. Leaf would just have to find them through trial and error. As she wheeled the bed along, she noticed a frozen TV at one of the nurse's stations. The corner of the screen said it was 11:57, and a video image of some news was paused mid-sentence. The newscaster's mouth was wide open and a frozen type crawl across the bottom said only *measures may include drastic.*

Once she got to the bottom floor, she saw it had long been deserted. It was dusty, there were cobwebs trailing from the ceiling, and only one in three ceiling light panels worked.

But there was also a faded sign on the wall, and color-coded trails on the floor, which she could just make out through the dust. The red trail was to the operating theaters and there was a blue trail to something euphemistically called "Survival Center," which was almost certainly the bomb shelter.

Leaf pushed the bed into the corridor, then left it to scout out where she should push it to, her running footsteps sending up clouds of dust as she raced along the corridor.

The Survival Center was a disappointment. It was definitely a bomb shelter, featuring a reinforced door with a hydraulic wheel to open and shut it. But it was way too small and could only ever have sheltered perhaps twenty people standing up. All its pipes and fittings had been removed as well, leaving ugly holes and hanging wires. Leaf figured she might be stuck wherever she was going to be for some time, and she didn't want that place to have no toilet or running water.

She raced on, flinging open doors. Most of the rooms were small and useless, but the operating theater complex was more promising. Though it had been cleared out, there were four big operating theaters clustered around a large central room that had several sinks with taps that worked, and there was a bathroom with at least one flushing toilet reached from the corridor outside.

Leaf propped the doors open and ran back to get her first bed-load. As she pushed the bed back to the theater complex, she wondered what on earth she was going to do. There was no way she could bring all the sleepers down here on beds. Even loading them up was very hard for her, given that nearly all of them were bigger than her, some of them weighed at least twice what she did, and their rigidity just added to the level of difficulty. She would be exhausted before she transported a dozen of them, even if she could do that before time restarted for everyone else.

I'll have to just pick out the smallest, she thought. *And do my best.*

"What have you gotten me into now, Arthur?" she said aloud. "And where have you gone?"

Chapter Fourteen

Arthur didn't feel a sudden shock of pain as he was mangled by the rising chain, and Alyse was still holding his hand, so he flipped back the peak of his cap and shook his head to get the water out of his eyes.

"Careful!" said Alyse. "No sudden moves. Grab hold of the ring, there."

They were standing in the chain link that was rapidly rising up through the middle of the stacked office units. Arthur grabbed the ring welded into the link's left inner wall, and Alyse let go of his hand to nonchalantly step over and hold the ring on the other side.

"Good view of one of the Drasils coming up," Alyse pointed out. "Or as good a view as you can get with the rain. Level 6222 is always empty, so you can see through it."

"Why is it empty?" asked Arthur. "And what's a Drasil?"

He was still wondering what the Will had tried to say, and why it had only spoken to him at that moment, and for such a brief time, so he forgot to put on the vacant, gormless expression of the recently washed-between-the-ears.

Alyse looked at him sharply before answering, but Arthur's mind was still on the Will and he didn't notice.

"Dunno why they're empty. There's empty offices from 6222 to 6300, at 6733 to 6800, and I've heard there's a bunch just below the top as well, whatever the top is now. It's probably near 61700, or something like that."

"Sixty one thousand seven hundred levels?" Arthur was paying attention now. "But each of the office cubes is about ten feet high, which would make the tower six hundred thousand feet high —"

"Nah, the levels just have a six in front for some reason. They start at sixty-one," said Alyse. "Tradition, I suppose. Depending on where the top has got to this week, it'll be about seventeen thousand feet. I'd love to see up there."

"We don't go up that far?" asked Arthur, somewhat reassured.

"Not yet, we haven't," said Alyse. "Other gangs do a bit up there. Most of the top construction work is done by automatons. Hey, triple two's coming up. Look that way."

Arthur stared out at the offices flashing by, blurred images of green lamps and different-colored umbrellas and Denizens in black or dark gray coats hunched over identical desks.

Then that view suddenly disappeared. Arthur could see the skeleton of the tower, empty office units that were just cubes of wrought iron, with exposed horizontal and vertical driving chains here and there, and the network of pneumatic message pipes. The view was broken in places by closed vertical shafts or walled-off rooms, but for the most part he could see through and out of the tower to the rain-swept sky beyond.

Far off in the distance, there was something he thought was another tower — a dark, vertical smudge on the horizon that went up and up until it disappeared into the sky.

"Good view of that Drasil today," said Alyse. "I wouldn't mind climbing one of them too, if it weren't for the insects."

"Insects?" Arthur didn't like the sound of that. He wanted to ask more about what a Drasil was, but he had finally noticed that Alyse was looking at him suspiciously, and he was wondering if he had pushed the washed-out memory excuse too far.

"Yes, Sunday's guard insects that patrol the Drasils. And the trees defend themselves too, I've heard. You know, now that you're clean, Ray, you don't look much like a Piper's child."

"I don't?" asked Arthur. The cascade of water had taken all the mud off his face.

"Nope." Alyse had her hand on her wrench, and her eyes behind her rain-washed goggles were very cold.

Arthur let his hand fall onto his own wrench, and he tensed a little, ready to draw.

"I reckon you must be some sort of short Denizen spy for the Big Boss. It's bad enough having the Sorcerous Supernumeraries following us about, without a spy among us. So it's time for you to —"

Arthur blocked her sudden swing at his legs with his own wrench. Sparks flew as the silver tools met. Alyse let go of the ring and struck again, a two-handed blow that would have overcome any normal Piper's child. Arthur met it one-handed, and it was Alyse who reeled back and would have fallen if Arthur hadn't hooked his foot around her ankle just before she went over.

"I'm not a spy!" Arthur shouted. "Or a Denizen!"

Alyse grabbed hold of the ring again and eyed him warily.

"What are you, then?"

"I'm Arthur, the Rightful Heir of the Architect. I've come here to find and free Part Six of the Will."

"No, you're not!" exclaimed Alyse. "Arthur's eight feet tall, and he's got a pointy beard down to his waist!"

"Those stupid books!" groaned Arthur. Some Denizen (or group of Denizens) somewhere in the House was writing and distributing very much fictionalized accounts of Arthur and his activities in the House. "Those books are all lies. I really am Arthur."

"You *are* very strong," said Alyse. "And you are more like us than a Denizen . . . no pointy beard, hey?"

"No."

"If you are Arthur, then you're an enemy of the Big Boss, right?"

"If you mean Superior Saturday, yes I am."

"Who doesn't trust us anymore, on account of the Piper being out and about again."

"Yes. Neither does Dame Primus — I mean, the Will of the Architect. The Parts I've already gathered, that is. But I trust you. I mean I trust Piper's children in general. In fact, I reckon the children are the smartest and most sensible people of anyone in the whole House."

"That's true," Alyse easily agreed. "But speaking for the gang, we don't care for politics. We just want to get our work done."

"I'm not going to interfere with your work," Arthur

promised. "Just don't report me. As soon as I can figure out where the Will is, we'll be off."

"That Suze who's with you — she really *is* a Piper's child, isn't she?"

"Yes." Out of the corner of his eye, Arthur saw that they had passed the empty office blocks, and the cubes were all full of green lamps and working Denizens again. Only here the umbrellas were all orange.

Alyse looked at Arthur thoughtfully.

"I suppose we could just go along with it for today," she said. "I mean, accept you for what you say you are. If there's any trouble, I'll act as surprised as anyone."

"That'd be great!" exclaimed Arthur. "I just need some time to track down the Will. I'll stay out of your way."

"Just do your work," said Alyse. "Otherwise it'll look suspicious. You can sneak out of the depot tonight. I want you gone before morning."

"Very well," said Arthur. "Hopefully I'll know where I need to go by then."

"You don't know where this Will is?"

"No. But the Will can speak inside my mind, tell me how to find it. I've already heard it twice. I heard it just before we got on this chain, when all that water splashed on my head."

"There's always a lot of splashes," said Alyse. "The full sorcerers, up above 61000, they like to play games, weave spell-nets to catch the rain and then let it all go at once on their inferiors below. Can be dangerous. We've lost a few workers, washed right out of an office and into a shaft, or even out of one side."

"It's odd," said Arthur. "This constant rain. I mean, the weather was broken in the Middle House, but it must be on purpose here, since Superior Saturday has all her sorcerers to fix it."

Alyse shrugged. "It's just the way it's always been," she said. "Least for the last ten thousand years. Same as when the Boss started building this tower."

"Ten thousand years?" asked Arthur. "It's been raining for ten thousand years in House time? How do you know? Haven't you been washed between the ears?"

"Course I have," said Alyse. "That's what the Denizens say. They're always talking about the plan, and building the tower, and how it's been ten thousand years, and if only the tower would reach the Gardens, then the rain will stop and all that. Look, there's the Drasil again — we're going through the seven hundreds."

"Reach the Gardens?" asked Arthur. "The Incomparable Gardens? That's what Saturday is trying to do?"

"That's what the sorcerers say. We just do our job. Can't be worrying about all the top-level stuff and plans and that."

"What is a Drasil?" Arthur looked through the empty, spare structure of the tower at the distant, vertical line.

"A very, very big tree. There's four Drasils. They hold up the Incomparable Gardens and they're always growing. I don't know how high they are, but everyone says the tower is not even close."

"Maybe the rain makes them grow," said Arthur.

"Maybe."

Arthur kept looking at the Drasil until they passed through the empty section and the view was once more obscured by thousands of offices. Alyse didn't talk, but that suited Arthur. He had a lot to think about.

The rain is important, he thought. *It must be, if it started ten thousand years ago, when the Trustees broke the Will. I wonder if it's Sunday who makes it rain, for the Drasil trees? But that couldn't be right, because Saturday has the Sixth Key, and it would be strongest here . . . only I kind of remember someone saying the Seventh Key was paramount or the strongest overall or something like that. . . .*

"We're coming up to the eight hundreds."

Alyse's voice interrupted Arthur's train of thought. He looked out and wondered how she knew what level they were at. Then he saw green umbrellas everywhere, in many different shades. The sorcerers, or would-be sorcerers, had umbrellas of dark green, bright emerald green, and lime green, as well as ones that had graduated washes of green and patterns of green.

"Green umbrellas in the eight hundreds," said Arthur. "That's how you know where we are — from the color change in the umbrellas."

"Yep," Alyse confirmed. "Yellow at nine hundred, then you count. There are numbers on the framework, but they're too small and hard to read from the Big Chain. Now get ready — we'll have to step off in a minute."

She took his hand again and they shuffled to the edge of the link. The offices were flashing past very swiftly, Arthur thought. Suddenly the umbrellas changed to yellow. He glanced at Alyse and saw her lips moving as she counted. He tried to count too, but couldn't keep up.

"Eighty-five — get ready!" snapped Alyse.

Arthur started counting again in his head.

"Ninety-four! Go!"

They stepped off the link, Alyse dragging Arthur, timing it to perfection so that it felt like no more dangerous than stepping down from a high curb.

"Move!" Alyse snapped again. Arthur followed her,

splashing past the desk and its oblivious Denizen under his yellow umbrella.

"Got to make room," explained Alyse as she led the way through to a neighboring office. Behind them, two more grease monkeys stepped off the link and quickly moved diagonally through to an adjacent office.

Arthur looked around and noticed that for the first time, the Denizens at their desks were covertly watching the grease monkeys. While most of them were continuing to write with both hands, they all slowed down to get a better sidelong look.

"Why are they watching us?" Arthur whispered to Alyse.

"Because they know we're here to shift someone up or *down*," said Alyse loudly. She glared at the Denizen behind the desk next to her. He immediately looked back at his shaving mirror screen and his writing sped up.

"Right," said Arthur. More grease monkeys stepped off the chain and one waved as they splashed their way across. It was Suzy, who looked like she was enjoying herself. He waved back, and learned that he shouldn't tip his head back when doing so, because a sheet of rain fell on his face.

Alyse had her notebook out again and was studying an entry, her finger moving along the lines. Arthur noticed that all the closer Denizens were watching intently despite Alyse's earlier glaring.

More grease monkeys arrived in pairs and moved through the offices, until the last, Whron, stepped off alone.

Alyse shut her notebook with a snap and pointed deeper into the tower.

"This way!" she declared.

"Is it a promotion?" asked a Denizen. He had given up all pretense of work, and was staring at Alyse, his mouth twisted up in an ugly expression that didn't match his handsome features.

Alyse ignored him. Striding through a waterfall that had just started coming down, she led the gang deeper into the tower, pausing every now and then to check the numbers that were embossed on the red iron posts that made up the framework of the building.

As the grease monkeys marched, Arthur heard the Denizens whispering all around them.

"Promotion . . . it must be . . . promotion . . . who is it . . . promotion . . . anyone see a purple capsule . . . promotion . . . promotion . . ."

"There she is, four offices ahead," Alyse whispered to Arthur. "With the saffron checks on the darker yellow. You wait here and join Whron — he'll tell you what to do. And look out."

"For what?" asked Arthur.

"The others will throw things as soon as they know it's a promotion. Wait for Whron now."

Arthur nodded and stopped where he was. Whron was close behind, and the other grease monkeys were approaching in an extended line across a dozen offices.

"Go!" shouted Alyse. She ran ahead to the chosen office, jumped on the desk, and then from there to a corner of the cube. Holding on to the frame with one hand, she started working on something with a wrench.

The Denizen stood up and folded her yellow umbrella. It turned black as it closed. Then, as she reopened it, a rich purple color spread in swirls across the fabric like oil in water. She propped the umbrella up, then quickly climbed under the desk, calling out as she did so.

"Good-bye, idiots! Long may you labor in vain!"

As the other grease monkeys swarmed over to the office, Arthur ran with Whron to the lower-left corner. Whron had his wrench out and started working on a large bolt that fastened the office cube to the framework. Arthur didn't know what he was supposed to do. He drew his wrench but only stood there until Whron looked up at him angrily.

"Come on! Get the other side!"

The restraining bolt went through the frame and was

fastened on the other side with a large hexagonal bronze nut. Arthur got his wrench onto it as Whron turned the bolt and drew it free.

Arthur caught the nut as it fell, just before it disappeared through the latticed floor.

"Next one up!" Whron called out, immediately going to another bolt a foot up from the first. Three other teams of grease monkeys were undoing the bolts in the other corners, and more were working above and around the office, some of them standing on each other's shoulders and some even hanging by their fingers from the latticed floor above, like real monkeys.

"Booklicker!" shouted a nearby Denizen.

"Toady!"

"Slithering sycophant!"

"You stole my promotion!"

All the Denizens in the nearer offices were shouting, waving their umbrellas, and becoming very obstreperous.

"Hurry!" snapped Whron. "They'll start throwing things in a second."

As Arthur crouched to get his wrench positioned, something hit him hard in the back and fell at his feet. He looked down and saw it was a broken teacup. Then a saucer smashed into pieces in front of his face, the debris falling on Whron's back.

"Lower East bolts clear!" shouted a grease monkey.

"Lower West bolts clear!"

"Lower North bolts clear!"

"Darn it," spat Whron. "Last. Got the nut? Lower South bolts clear!"

His declaration was echoed by the teams working on the ceiling and by shouts that came from higher up. Arthur looked and saw that there were other gangs on the higher floors, and, amid them, several dull bronze automatons that looked like ambulatory jellyfish, round three-foot-diameter globes that stood five feet tall and walked on four or five semirigid tentacles while they wielded tools in their other numerous appendages.

"Check chain!" shouted Alyse.

Whron used the edge of his wrench to peel back what Arthur had thought was a solid part of the vertical frame but was in fact a red-painted cover or lid that fit snugly on the beam. Under it, there was a smaller version of the Big Chain, big fat links four or five times the size of a bicycle chain. The chain ran on the inside of the U-shaped vertical beam, though it was not moving now.

"Chain present — looks all right!"

Diagonally opposite, another grease monkey confirmed that the chain was present there.

Alyse looked up, cupped her hands around her mouth, and shouted, "Ready to rise! Shift them aside!"

Arthur looked up too, completely in the moment, all his troubles and responsibilities forgotten, replaced by curiosity as he wondered what exactly was going to shift aside.

Chapter Fifteen

The offices above Arthur creaked and rattled, then a whole line of them started to slowly move to the right, like carriages on a train being shunted off from a station. The next level up again, other offices were moving away in a different direction, and on the next level above that, and above that, presumably all the way up to level 61012, seventeen floors above.

As the vertical gap appeared that would allow the promoted Denizen's office to ascend, the barrage of cups, saucers, and inkwells slowed and then stopped, as did the stream of abuse. But a lot more water started coming down, more than could be explained by the constant rain, and Arthur saw brief, hallucinatory images of giant buckets woven out of purple light that were upending themselves into the new, temporary shaft.

"Stand clear!" ordered Alyse. "Not you, Ray. You stay with me. The rest of you, take the Big Chain to 61012."

"Hey, I want to go up in this —" Suzy started to say, before Arthur made a gesture with his hand against his throat. She scowled, looked at Alyse, who met her eyes with an unflinching gaze, and then reluctantly followed the others back to the Big Chain.

Arthur moved to the middle of the office, ducked sideways to avoid a huge splash of water from above, and stood next to the desk, which still had the Denizen under it. She looked at Arthur and sniffed.

"Take it up!" shouted Alyse. An automaton waved a tentacle in reply, and a few seconds later, the office shook as the chains in the framework clanked into motion. Slowly, with a juddering screech, the office began to rise up toward its destination.

As it rose, a huge sheet of water came crashing down, so much that it couldn't run off fast enough, creating a temporary puddle as deep as Arthur's knees.

Arthur! I am spread throughout the —

It was the voice of Part Six of the Will.

"What was that?" asked a voice from under the desk. "I smell sorcery!"

The Denizen poked her head out and sniffed the air, but quickly withdrew again when another great dump of water splashed across her face.

Arthur shook his head, sending a spray of droplets to join the rain.

Alyse looked at him suspiciously.

"Everything's fine," said Arthur brightly. He lifted his wrench. "All ready to get back to work."

"Be sure you are," Alyse replied.

Spread throughout . . . the what? thought Arthur. *The Will has spoken to me three times now, the last two times when I've just been soaked. . . .*

"The rain," Arthur whispered to himself. He tucked his wrench under his arm, held his hands together, and held them out, watching the rain splash and fill his makeshift cup. Soon brimming over, he held his hands up under the green lamp on the desk, searching the clear water for an indication that he had guessed correctly.

Under the light, deep in the liquid, Arthur saw letters loop and twine, forming words that he knew well, breaking apart and forming again in a constant struggle against the fluid medium.

Part Six of the Will is in the rain. Broken across thousands — maybe millions — of raindrops. It's only able to come together a bit when water gathers. Like in that drain, or a big splash from above. . . .

"What are you doing, Piper's child?" asked the Denizen, who had once again come out from under her desk. She bent under her umbrella and lifted the pince-nez spectacles that hung from a cord around her neck.

"I thought I saw something fall," said Arthur. "I caught it, but it must have been a piece of bread or something that fell apart."

"Really?" asked the Denizen. She settled the pince-nez on her nose and blinked. "I thought I smelled sorcery . . . and now I see there is something in your pouch. Give it to me."

Arthur slowly shook his head and stepped closer, his wrench in his hand.

"Ray . . ." warned Alyse.

"Give it to me before I blast you to tiny shreds," said the Denizen in a bored voice. "I am a full sorcerer now, albeit only of the Fifth Grade for the moment. Hand it over!"

Her hand went to the umbrella, ready to fold and wield it.

Arthur struck as her fingers pressed the catch and the umbrella began to fold. His wrench bounced off the Denizen's head. She blinked once and said, "No little Piper's child can hit hard enough to . . . to . . ."

She blinked again and slowly slid to the floor. Arthur, keeping them both covered and out of sight under the partly folded umbrella, shoved her back under the desk.

"What have you done!" exclaimed Alyse in a furious whisper. "You'll get us all executed!"

"I only knocked her out," said Arthur. "It had to be done. Tell me, is there somewhere all this rain goes? Like a big stormwater reservoir or something?"

"What?" asked Alyse. She peered under the desk and then looked back up. Her gang was already above, but so were a line of sad-eyed Sorcerous Supernumeraries.

"How did they get ahead of us?" asked Arthur.

"They caught a normal elevator like they always do!"

"They'll wonder what's happened to this sorcerer, won't they?"

"Of course they will!"

"Do the Denizens ever sleep at their desks?" Arthur asked. He was trying to think how to hide the sorcerer, but there wasn't anywhere completely out of sight. They were surrounded by sorcerers at their desks, thousands of them. . . .

"They always sleep at their desks," said Alyse. "But it's not nighttime, is it? I knew I should have pushed you off the Big Chain!"

They were four floors away from their destination now. Arthur could see Suzy leaning over the edge, watching him. She waved again. Arthur responded by scratching his cap in an agitated way and throwing his hands up in the air, hoping that this might send a message that they were about to be in serious trouble. Not that there was anything Suzy could do.

All he could think of was to take out the Fifth Key, destroy as many of the Sorcerous Supernumeraries and the surrounding sorcerers in their offices as he could in a surprise attack, and then use the Key to escape. But that wouldn't free the Will, and it would be very difficult to get back, even now that he'd seen the place and could use the Key, since there were all these sorcerers who would be watching for just such a thing.

"Have you ever had one keep hiding under a desk after they've risen up?" he asked Alyse.

"Of course not! Some of them have been waiting thousands of years to get promoted. They get out and dance on their desks half the time. Or start weaving spells to catch water and throw it down on their former fellows."

Three floors away and there were more Sorcerous Supernumeraries staring mournfully down and shuffling on the edge of the temporary shaft.

"Right," said Arthur. He quickly looked around to check that the office was above the eyeline of the Denizens around them. "I'd better do something."

"What?" asked Alyse.

"This," said Arthur, and he shifted the umbrella so he

and part of the desk were hidden from the sight of the Denizens above.

Alyse looked puzzled, an expression that changed to horror as Arthur suddenly reached out with his wrench and smashed the green desk lamp. It exploded with a vicious crack and a shower of sparks. A sheet of flame shot up, and the rain falling on it created an instant pall of steam.

Moving through the cloud, Arthur sprang to the corner and stuck his wrench into the rising chain. Exerting all his unnatural strength, he tried to break one of the links open, but the wrench bent in half and snapped off in his hand. The chain kept rising with the broken head in it, and the office kept rising too . . . for about half a foot. Then there was a fearful screeching, and the office suddenly lurched up on one side and down on the other. Arthur, Alyse, the desk, and the unconscious Denizen began to slide off into an adjacent office.

"Shut down!" Alyse screamed up the shaft as she kicked the desk to push it against a corner. "Chain break! Shut down! Chain break!"

Still obscured by steam, Arthur stopped the Denizen's slide, but the office was continuing to rise on the far side, tilting the floor even more.

"Shut it down!" Alyse continued to shout.

The chain suddenly stopped its mechanical shriek, the office juddered to a full stop at a thirty-degree angle, the flame from the green lamp sputtered out, and the steam wafted away. Arthur quickly arranged the Denizen against the jammed up desk, so she looked like she'd struck her head in the accident.

"Who would know where the water goes?" Arthur asked Alyse with some urgency.

"How dare you!" was Alyse's reply. "We had such a good record!"

"Some things are more important," said Arthur coldly. "Like the fact that the whole House and the entire Universe is going to be destroyed unless I do something. So stop whining and tell me who might know where all the storm-water goes!"

Alyse grimaced and looked up, rain tapping on her goggles. Then she looked back at Arthur.

"Dartbristle would know. Go ask him, and get away from us!"

"You all right down there?" called a grease monkey from above.

"Not exactly!" shouted Arthur. "Just give us a minute!"

"Where would I find Dartbristle?" Arthur continued in a quiet tone. "Also, I bet we need a pass or something to go back by ourselves, right?"

"There's a pennywhistle by the drain you came up," said Alyse. "Play his tune on that and he'll come to the depot."

"His tune? Oh, yeah, the one he whistles — I remember that."

Arthur had a very good musical ear, so good that people often assumed that he'd inherited it from his father, the lead singer of The Ratz, not knowing that Bob was actually his adoptive father.

"Do we need a pass to go back?"

"I'll write to say you're going to fetch a part we need." Alyse got out her book and a blue pencil and quickly scribbled something on a page. Then she tore out the page and handed it to Arthur, saying, "That's it. Just go!"

"Everything's going to change," Arthur told her. "Whether you want it to or not. The only question is whether the change is for the better or the worse."

"We just want to do our job," said Alyse, repeating the words like a mantra.

The umbrella above them suddenly moved, a black-clad Sorcerous Supernumerary sweeping it aside. Another Supernumerary landed with a splash next to him, and then a third jumped down. They ignored Arthur and Alyse, going to look at the unconscious sorcerer on the floor. Each of them, Arthur noticed, had the slightest of smiles that would not be visible to anyone farther away than he and Alyse. They were pleased to see an unconscious sorcerer and a halted promotion.

"Boss? What do we do?" a grease monkey called from above.

Alyse looked up. "Get yourself down here! You and Bigby and Whron. I'm sending Ray and Suze back down to get a Number Three temporary chain bracket. The rest of you, I want every inch of horizontal chain from here to ten offices out in all directions checked for corrosion."

"Corrosion accident causal effect?" asked a tinny, booming voice.

The speaker was one of the octopoidal automatons. It spoke through a valve under its central sphere, which rather horribly opened and shut as it talked.

"How would I know?" shouted Alyse. "Most likely, though. We'll have to look."

"Higher authority approaches," reported the automaton. "Await instruction."

"Big nob!" hissed one of the grease monkeys above.

The three Sorcerous Supernumeraries straightened like string puppets yanked to attention and rapidly climbed back up.

"Quick, you drop over the side to the next level, run through to the north side, and use your wings," Alyse told

Arthur. "A Sorcerer-Overseer will see who you are straight away, up close."

"Suze!" Arthur shouted. "Get down here!"

He slid down the uneven floor and began to lower himself over the side, making sure first that he wasn't going to drop on the head of the Denizen below.

"Thanks," Arthur said to Alyse. "Suze! Come on!"

"I'm here!" Suzy called, landing with a thump near Arthur and almost rolling off before she got a good handhold. "In a hurry, are we?"

"Yes," said Arthur. He let go and dropped down to the next floor. He'd thought of aiming for the desk so he didn't have so far to fall, but decided against it. There was no point in attracting the attention of the sorcerer there, particularly since he'd just noticed that these Denizens with the purple umbrellas weren't writing. They still looked into the shaving mirror viewers or whatever they were, but they weren't writing anything.

"Where we going?" asked Suzy.

"To the side and down," Arthur said quietly as he led the way through an office and dodged around the occupant, who had pushed his chair back much farther than normal. "Flying. We have to find Dartbristle again and get him to lead us to wherever the stormwater goes."

"Why not just ask Alyse? She's got that guide to the whole place and all."

Arthur stopped suddenly and Suzy ran into his back.

"What guide?" he asked.

"That book — it's got maps and instructions and everything, for wherever the gang might have to go," said Suzy. "Least that's what Bigby was telling me. Kind of like your Atlas, only not as good."

Arthur looked back. They'd only gone half a dozen offices.

"She just wanted to get rid of us," he said.

"Fair enough," said Suzy. "Can't blame her for that."

"Yes, I can." Arthur was about to say more when a huge torrent of water crashed down between him and Suzy, knocking the Piper's child off her feet.

"This 'ere rain is a bit much," Suzy said as she struggled to her feet. "Wouldn't mind a bit of sunshine, meself."

"Wouldn't we all," said the Denizen at the nearby desk. He didn't look away from his mirror-screen.

"Thought you lot weren't supposed to talk to us," Suzy chided.

"We're not," sighed the sorcerer. "But it gets so boring just watching the mirror, waiting for something worth watching. What was that you were saying about someone wanting to get rid of you? I couldn't hear properly over the rain."

"It was nothing," said Arthur.

"Just the usual?" The Denizen sighed again. "I thought you grease monkeys weren't so afflicted, not being eligible for promotion and so forth."

"Afflicted?" asked Suzy.

"Resentful and envious," said the Denizen. "Take my last promotion, for example. The fellows I'd drunk tea with for the last thousand years, shared many a biscuit . . . they threw our department silver teapot at me as I rose above their heads."

"Come on, Suze," said Arthur. "We need to go back up."

"We do? What about that Overseer?"

"An Overseer?" squeaked the Denizen. "Get away from me! I must attend to my studies!"

He immediately opened a book and began to read it quietly aloud while also watching his mirror, one eye focused left and one focused right, which was quite disturbing to see.

Arthur stood still for a minute, thinking, then started back toward the stalled office.

"What about that Overseer?" Suzy asked again in a whisper as she caught up with him.

"If we keep our distance, we should be fine," Arthur assured her. He was so mad at Alyse that he didn't even consider the potential danger of being discovered. "I'll get the information we need from Alyse and we'll go again."

Four grease monkeys were working on the broken office, but Alyse herself was not there and neither were the unconscious sorcerer, the Sorcerous Supernumeraries, or any other Denizens. Arthur watched for a few seconds to make sure the coast was clear, then climbed up the corner framework and back into the office.

Whron looked over from where he was undoing a chain link.

"I thought Alyse sent you to get a chain bracket!"

"She did," said Arthur. "But I have to check something with her first. Where is she? With the Sorcerer-Overseer?"

"What Overseer?" asked Whron. "There was an Automaton-Scheduler, but that's like five . . . four ranks below . . ."

"Where's Alyse, then?"

"Dunno." Whron shrugged. "Everyone's checking the chain up on the next floor, except for us."

"Right!" said Arthur. Flexing his knees, he jumped to the top of the desk, which had been tipped up to get it out of the way. From there, he jumped again to the next floor, a leap of at least eight feet.

"Show-off," grumbled Suzy, and climbed up the corner.

Chapter Sixteen

Alyse was one office away on the next level, rolling up a piece of paper to put in the message capsule that was on the sorcerer's desk. All the other grease monkeys were busy inspecting chains, spread out through all the offices around. There was no sign of the automatons or the Automaton-Scheduler.

Arthur bounded over to Alyse and grabbed her elbow, turning her around so their backs were toward the sorcerer.

"You tried to trick me," whispered Arthur fiercely. "Your handbook has the information I need."

"Let go of me!" Alyse protested, but she was whispering too.

"Don't make a fuss," warned Arthur, tightening his grip on her arm. "If they find out who I am, then the whole gang will be punished . . . maybe even executed."

"All right," said Alyse. "What do you want?"

"I want to find a large reservoir or water store. But first I want to see that message."

He reached over and took the paper before Alyse could snatch it away, and flicked it open one-handed.

To Senior Shift-Sorcerer 61580

Report two suspicious Piper's children flying down to Grease Monkey Depot of 27th Chain and Motivation Maintenance Brigade. Calling themselves Ray and Suze.

"You traitor!" spat Arthur.

"Is that message ready or not?" asked the sorcerer. He was unperturbed by the obvious animosity between Arthur and Alyse. "I haven't got all day."

"There's been a mistake," said Arthur. "No message, thanks."

He forced Alyse toward the temporary shaft and handed the message to Suzy, whose face clouded as she read it.

"Us Piper's children always stick together," whispered Suzy. "Always!"

"The job comes first," said Alyse.

"You hold her, Suzy, while I look up her book," Arthur instructed. "Act casual. Alyse — remember that if you try anything, the whole gang will cop it, one way or another."

"What do you mean, act casual?" asked Suzy as she took Alyse's other arm.

"Act like you're friends looking at something on the floor together," said Arthur. He opened Alyse's pocket and took out her handbook.

"It won't work for you," said Alyse. "Gang bosses only."

"It had better work for me," Arthur said as he opened it up. Alyse gasped.

"But you can't open it!"

Arthur ignored her and read the title page: *Chain and Motivation Maintenance Guide Registered No. 457589.*

Arthur flipped to the back. There was an index that just listed the capital letters A–Z. Arthur touched the W and the pages flipped to show a list of topics that began with that letter. He read through them quickly, until he saw *Water*, which had a long list of subtopics, including *Storage facilities, permanent* and *Storage facilities, transient.*

Under *Water, Storage facilities, permanent,* there were several listings, including *Central Rain Reservoir* and *Midtower Rain Booster Tank*. Arthur didn't even need to touch the latter topic; he just looked at it longer than any other line, and the pages immediately flipped to show a cutaway drawing, a map, and a list of technical details.

"There's a water store up higher; it's about a hundred offices square and sits between 61350 and 61399," Arthur said. "That'll probably do — it must be big enough."

"Big enough for what?" asked Suzy, who was crouched down with Alyse, both of them apparently intent on the latticed floor.

"I'll tell you on the way." Arthur checked the handbook again, closed it, and was about to put it in his pocket when it shook in his hand and made a rattling noise.

"What's that mean?"

"Change of orders," said Alyse. "Please, can I check it?"

Arthur hesitated. At that moment, he heard a sudden hiss and rattle erupt from everywhere around, followed a second later by the pop of capsules ejecting from the pneumatic message tubes and clattering onto every Denizen's desk within sight.

Arthur opened the handbook, which went straight to a page that said in large, red type:

GENERAL MOBILIZATION!
The tower has reached the target point underside of the Incomparable Gardens. All engineering gangs are to report immediately to Ground Floor Exterior Platform Lift One under the command of Saturday's Noon to secure and lift the assault ram.

Arthur looked around. Every single Denizen was standing up, and they were all removing and furling their umbrellas. Those who already had their umbrellas in hand were stepping out to form up in long files, facing deeper into the tower, ready to march,

"Are the normal elevators that way?" Arthur asked Alyse.

"Yes," she said. "What are the orders? We must obey!"

Arthur gave her the handbook. As Alyse read, he looked around. The leader of the Sorcerous Supernumeraries was reading a similar book to Alyse's. The Supernumerary looked up and her sad gaze met Arthur's. He quickly looked down, just in case she was powerful enough to recognize who — or what — he was.

"We have to get going!" repeated Alyse. "This is it, the big one. We'll get to ride the cage all the way to the top!"

"What's this assault ram?" asked Arthur.

Alyse shrugged. "Something big enough that it needs to go up on the outside cargo elevator. It's amazing — three hundred feet a side and no chain. It's self-propelling, driven by ten score senior sorcerers —"

"Can we ride up on that too?" asked Suzy, fired by Alyse's enthusiasm.

"No," Arthur said decisively. "Alyse, I'll let you and

the gang go, but you have to promise that you won't tell and won't betray us."

"Sure! Fine!" said Alyse, a little too quickly.

Arthur looked around. The closer sorcerers were marching away. Only the Sorcerous Supernumeraries were still close, and they were watching the grease monkeys, who were mostly only pretending to inspect chains while they looked at Alyse and waited for her to tell them what was going on.

"Give me your hand," he said quickly and quietly. "And promise me, Lord Arthur, Rightful Heir of the Architect, that you will not betray us."

Alyse took Arthur's hand.

"I promise you, Lord Arthur, that I won't betray you."

A faint glow left Arthur's fingers and moved into Alyse's hand. She cried out, but Arthur didn't let her go until the faint light had disappeared.

"What occurs?" asked a slow, deep voice.

Arthur looked around. One of the Sorcerous Supernumeraries had sidled closer and was sniffing the air.

"Something shiny fell down from above and went across the floor somewhere," Arthur said hastily. "But I guess there's no time to look for it, what with this general mobilization and all, right, boss?"

"Yes," said Alyse slowly. She shook her head vigorously, sending a spray of water across Arthur's and Suzy's faces. "No time to waste . . ."

"Something from above? Something *shiny*?" asked the Supernumerary. He immediately knelt down and started sniffing the floor. Arthur and the others moved away.

"No time to waste!" shouted Alyse. "Form up, gang! We're going down to the floor to work on Outside Elevator Number One!"

"Number One?" came a shouted question from the tilted office below. "Outside Elevator Number One?"

"Yes!" yelled Alyse. "Come on! Back to the Big Chain!"

The Supernumerary started to sniff toward Arthur's feet. More of the funereal Denizens were coming over, intent on what their sniffing companion was doing.

"We'll take the up chain when the first two take the down chain," said Arthur as he and Suzy hurried after Alyse. All the offices were empty now, the Denizens and their umbrellas gone. "Get to this water store, get Part Six of the Will, and get out of here."

"What about this 'ere ram thing and old Saturday gettin' into the Gardens and everything?" asked Suzy.

"First things first," said Arthur. The Big Chain was only a dozen offices ahead. He looked back. All the Supernumeraries were on the floor of the office where he'd been — a big, ugly pile of black-clad Denizens all trying to sniff at the floor. They reminded him of the writhing piles of sawfly larvae that fell from the trees in the garden at home.

I hope I can get back in time to make sure I have a home, he thought. *Though people are more important than places, and the house is probably far enough away to survive that nuke attack. But Leaf and everyone — they're too close, and I don't even know what I've done or how long it will last. I can't think about it now. I have to concentrate on what's in front of me. . . .*

"What color umbrellas do they have in the 61300s?" asked Arthur. "If they haven't gone . . ."

"Checks of blue and yellow," said Alyse.

"We'll have to count from here," said Arthur as he looked up through the structure. He could see lines of moving Denizens, but they had their umbrellas furled and there were none still at their desks. "You start heading down, Alyse. We'll go around to the up chain."

"No hard feelings," said Alyse.

"Speak for yourself," Arthur replied.

I will return and punish her dreadfully, he thought, then suppressed the brief moment of rage. *There are more important things to do. Forget about it.*

"Wotcher, Alyse," said Suzy. "Don't get yer spanner in a twist!"

She waved cheerily as Alyse and another grease monkey stepped out and into a moving link of the downward chain. Arthur hurried around to stand on the edge next to the rising chain.

"Easy does it," said Suzy. Arthur took her hand and they both stood there for a few moments, watching the chain speed upward, gauging when they should step on.

"Now!" said Suzy, and they stepped forward. Either Suzy wasn't as good at judging the speed as Alyse, or Arthur was worse with his eyes open than his eyes shut, because they mistimed it a little and were flung about. One of Arthur's feet trailed over the side before he got his balance and hastily pulled it in.

"Oopsie-daisy," said Suzy. "This is a bit of fun, this chain. We could do with one of these back in the old Lower House, I reckon."

"There is no more Lower House," said Arthur. He was trying to count the floors as they whizzed past.

"That's right," said Suzy. "I forgot. Oh, well."

Arthur stared at her. How could she have forgotten that so easily? Sometimes he thought the Piper's children were no more human than the Denizens, no matter that they'd started out as mortal kids.

Thinking about that made him forget to count.

"Drat! I suppose it won't matter if we're a few floors out. The Rain Booster Tank is huge, according to that guidebook. Which I should have kept."

"Why do we want to go to a Rain Booster Tank?"

"Catch some of this rain and take a very close look." Arthur cupped his hand to demonstrate, and Suzy followed suit, being careful not to stick her hand out too far beyond the chain, where it might get lopped off by a protrusion from an upper floor.

"What am I looking for?" she asked when her hand was brimful of clear water.

"Letters and words," said Arthur.

"Yes! I see 'em!" exclaimed Suzy. "O-r-l-g-w-x-s-t-r-e . . . orlgwxstre . . . hmmm . . . that sounds familiar but I can't quite put me finger on —"

"It's not an actual word!" said Arthur. "It's just a random, jumbled-up bit of the Will. It's split up among all these raindrops. That's why I need to find a place where lots of water comes together, because more, or even most, of the Sixth Part of the Will should be there."

"Right!" Suzy nodded. "So you get it and we get out?"

"Probably. I guess that's still the most sensible thing to do, though I wish I knew why Saturday wants to get into the Incomparable Gardens, and why she can't just go up an elevator. Oh, no!"

"What!?" Suzy looked around wildly.

"I've lost count again. Maybe we'll be able to see it, if the offices are empty."

All the offices they had been passing were empty, but a flash of movement caught Arthur's eye a few floors up.

"That one was full — but they were standing at their desks, not sitting."

"So's this one. What are they doing?"

The floors went by too quickly for Arthur to be sure, but as far as he could see, the offices they'd just passed were full of Denizens doing something that looked like tai chi — a formalized, slow dance, in their case performed at the side of their desks. Their umbrellas were furled too, so they were dancing in the rain, kicking up arcs of spray as they slowly turned and jumped.

"I have no idea what they're doing," said Arthur. He frowned and added, "I'd hoped all the Denizens would have gone off to the elevators, to head wherever they're going. Keep an eye out for anything that might look like a water reservoir. We must be getting close."

They went up past several more floors of sorcerers dancing at their desks, then there were more vacated floors, some with distant views of marching sorcerers heading off farther into the interior of the tower.

"You look that way, I'll look the other," Arthur said. "I've gotten confused about which way is north. I really should have kept that guidebook. I don't know what I was thinking."

"That Alyse needed it?" asked Suzy. "Zounds! Is that it?"

Arthur spun around, which was not a good thing to do when traveling quite fast inside the link of a vast, moving chain. He nearly lost his balance, and fell against Suzy, who staggered into the side of the link and almost lost her grip on the ring.

Recovering his stance, Arthur saw a glass wall some distance inside the tower, a glass wall that shimmered blue from the water inside it. The wall and the water continued up as they rose through the next floor, and the next.

"Do we keep going?" asked Suzy.

"To the top of it," answered Arthur, who was

counting very intently now. "Get ready, it's forty-nine floors high."

They stepped off at the forty-ninth floor, expecting to see either empty offices or offices with working sorcerers. But the office units here were not furnished with desks. Each ten-by-ten-foot office had a small lounge in it, and a standing lamp. The lounges were covered in different fabrics, ranging from black leather to bright floral patterns, and the standing lamps had matching shades.

"Artful Lounger territory," whispered Suzy.

"Yep," said Arthur. He looked around keenly. "But there aren't any here."

He started off towards the water tank. Though the rain obscured his view, he could see the clear glass wall of the tank through several floors, and the open top of it up ahead, with its rain-dappled surface of clean blue water. It looked like an enormous aquarium, and Arthur wondered if there were fish in it. Or other things . . .

"So do yer just stick your hand in, or what?" asked Suzy as they reached the edge of the huge tank and looked across the expanse of water.

We're ten thousand feet up a tower, and this water "tank" is about five hundred feet deep, thought Arthur, *with a surface area that's about equal to sixteen Olympic pools. That's some water storage!*

He bent down and dipped his hand in the water. Immediately he felt Part Six of the Will speak directly into his mind.

Arthur! I need your help to gather myself. Come into the water! There is no time to lose!

Chapter Seventeen

"It wants me to go into the water," Arthur told Suzy. He looked at the rain splashes and then back at the empty lounges behind them.

"So it's here?" Suzy asked. She kept looking back too.

"Yes," said Arthur. "I suppose I'd better go in. You keep watch."

Suzy nodded and drew her wrench, slapping the heavy adjustable head against her open hand.

Five hundred feet deep, thought Arthur. *That's waaaay too deep . . . but I have to get the Will.*

Steeling himself, Arthur slid off the latticed iron floor and into the water. It was cold, but not as cold as he'd expected. It was definitely not as cold as it should have been that high up, but then neither was the air. Saturday might like the rain, but she clearly didn't want the cold of an earthly high altitude.

Good! the Will chimed in. *Swim to the middle and call me!*

Arthur trod water for a few minutes. He'd done life-saving classes, and had swum in his clothes before, but not with his boots on. He was about to kick them off, but decided not to. He wasn't having any trouble staying afloat. Possibly because he wasn't having any trouble breathing, and his strength and endurance were far greater than they'd ever been.

He struck out for the middle, using the breaststroke rather than freestyle so he could see where he was going. It was slower, but safer. Halfway there, he rolled over on his back and did some backstroke so he could see Suzy. She waved, and he waved back.

Good work, Arthur! Now, call me with your mind.

Arthur trod water and watched the rain, visualizing the tiny fragments of the Will that lay inside each raindrop.

Part Six of the Will of the Architect, attend upon me, Arthur the Rightful Heir, he thought, his brow furrowed in concentration. *Join together and come to me!*

Long threads of type began to glow and flow through the water, twining together like the tendrils of luminous sea plants. The rain shone with an inner light and began to drive towards Arthur rather than falling straight down through the latticework floors. Up above him, drips and drops that had been caught on the floors sprang into motion, rolling and spreading to the nearest gap to fall again.

Sixty floors below Arthur, a sorcerer stared at her

mirror in amazement. She hesitated for a moment, then opened a small, secret drawer in the middle of her desk and depressed a dusty bronze button.

Around her, mirrors flashed. Denizens who had been paying scant attention leaned forward, snapping books shut and dropping pens. Above their heads, the pneumatic message tubes suddenly puffed and coughed, and red capsules began to fall upon the desks.

On the floors where the sorcerers danced, they all stopped in mid-beat. Umbrellas were snapped open, chairs dragged back as they sat down, and thousands of small mirrors were turned for better viewing.

Higher up the tower, as high as you could get for now, until the assault ram was raised, a telephone rang and was picked up by a milk-white, silky hand.

Arthur watched the threads of type weave themselves through the water, and he kept calling the Will inside his head. Slowly, the lines of type began to take on a shape, the shape of a large bird. It turned a dark color, a shining black, and its beak, head, and ruffled neck rose up out of the water.

"Good, Lord Arthur," croaked the raven. One text-wrought wing fluttered above the surface, while the other was still unformed threads of type. "I am almost complete. A little more rain must fall and be gathered in."

"Arthur!"

Arthur looked back to Suzy. She was pointing with her wrench.

"Artful Loungers! Lots of them!"

"A few more minutes," said the raven. "Keep calling me, Lord Arthur!"

Arthur tried to jump up so he could see what Suzy saw, but even with his hardest kicking he could only just raise up seven inches or so. But that was enough. All around the offices beyond the reservoir, Artful Loungers were crawling out from *under* the lounges. They had been there all along, hidden and quiescent.

Now they were advancing on Suzy, with their curved blue-steel swords and Nothing-poison stilettos of crystal.

Suzy flicked her rain-mantle behind her back and raised her wrench.

"Concentrate, Arthur! Call me!" said Part Six.

Arthur dove forward and broke into his fastest free-style stroke.

"Arthur! I can't escape without you!"

Arthur ignored the raven and swam faster, piercing the water like a dolphin. But even though he was swimming faster than he ever had, after a dozen strokes he was no closer to the side, and after a dozen more, he felt himself being pulled very strongly back. Rolling over, he was pushed sideways as well. As he swirled about, he felt a powerful tug at his ankles.

He was in a whirlpool. The water was running out of the tank, and he was going with it.

"Suzy!" yelled Arthur. The water had sunk so quickly and he was being twirled around so fast that he could only see Suzy's head. "Use your wings. Fly aw —"

Water filled his mouth. Flailing wildly, Arthur barely managed to get himself above the surface again. The suction was incredible, the action of tons and tons of water drawn into a ten-thousand-foot-high drain. Desperately he looked back, but he couldn't see Suzy, only the glitter of Artful Lounger swords, and through water-filled ears he heard the crash of metal and shouts and a single, cut-off scream.

Then he could only think of himself. He was drowning, his lungs filling with water as he was inexorably dragged below the surface. All his fears of a long, slow underwater death were coming true.

He scrabbled at his belt pouch, thrusting his fingers in to touch the Fifth Key through the bag, not trying to get it out, for if he did, he knew he would lose it for sure. He felt its power, weak though it was through the shielding metalcloth, and focused his mind to use its sorcery, only to be flung around so violently that his arms were twisted behind him and he was upended, diving headfirst down the drain.

Water completely filled his lungs and the last, pathetic bubble of air left his mouth.

I refuse to die, thought Arthur. *I am no longer human. I am the Rightful Heir of the Architect. I am going to breathe the water.*

He opened his mouth and took a deep, refreshing intake of water. All his choking sensations vanished, and his mouth, twisted moments ago in a panicked, silent scream, smoothed into something that was not quite a smile. He took another breath of water and pirouetted so he was upright, rushing feetfirst rather than headfirst down what must be an enormous pipe.

Suzy was probably only taken prisoner, he told himself. *I'll survive this and rescue her. It will be all right. . . .*

The water rushing him down suddenly changed direction. Arthur hit something very, very hard. He screamed, but no sound came out, just a blast of water from his mouth. Then he was picked up again and slammed even harder, bumping and scraping as the water surged and corkscrewed, carrying him with it.

Still screaming, Arthur curled up into a ball to protect himself — and, like a ball, was swept on and on, down and along the huge stormwater pipe that switchbacked its way through and down ten thousand feet.

It took half an hour for the water to reach the bottom. In that time, Arthur was smashed a hundred times against the sides of the pipe. He hurt terribly, all over, but the awful passage that would have killed any mortal at its beginning did not kill him.

At the bottom, the huge pipe spat out a waterfall that cascaded into a vast, under-floor lake, carved out of the bulwark rock under the Upper House. Arthur fell through the waterfall, sank to the bottom, and just lay there until the pains that wracked him diminished from the level of blinding stabs to a steady, debilitating ache.

It still hurt to move, but Arthur forced himself to swim up to the surface. Breaking out of the water, he was afraid he might not be able to breathe air, but he could, and it felt no different from when he was breathing the water.

Arthur wearily treaded water and looked around. He could see the huge pipe and the waterfall that still cascaded from it, but little else. There was fog, or steam, obscuring everything. As the water drained from his ears, he became aware of sound, the dull, repetitive thud of mighty engines.

Back under the floor, he thought. *In the middle of a lot of water. Must be the Central Rain Reservoir . . .*

"Part Six?" Arthur croaked. "Will. Are you here too?"

A raven head emerged from the water, but it was not glossy and black, and there were blank lines where parts of it were missing. It opened its beak and croaked, "Most of me is here, Lord Arthur, but some fragments are yet to arrive. In fact, I believe the few paragraphs that make up my tail are still falling as rain and will not arrive here for an hour or more."

"I doubt we've got an hour," said Arthur. "I was over-confident. Scamandros warned me that they could track any sorcery I did. I just didn't think calling you would count."

"Saturday must have devoted a very large number of her Denizens to watch for any signs of sorcery," said the Will. "It is surprising, since she is also massing her forces to assault the Incomparable Gardens. If we are fortunate, that battle will have commenced and will serve as a distraction. In any case, we are a long way under the floor here, and her servants do not like to venture into this region."

"The Rat-catcher automatons do, though," said Arthur. "Can you pull yourself together from anywhere in this pool?"

"Why, yes," said the Will. "Why?"

"You can do it from near solid ground, then. I have to get out of the water. I feel like I've been run over by a mammoth. Which way is the closest shore?"

"Follow me," said the raven head, and it began to move away. It looked quite horrible, just the head of a bird and part of its neck, gliding across the water without obvious means of propulsion.

Arthur swam slowly and wearily behind it, thinking about Suzy and Leaf. He felt as if he'd abandoned both of them, but he hadn't meant to. It was just how things had worked out.

Not that that's an excuse, he thought gloomily. *Maybe Suzy's okay — they probably just took her prisoner. And maybe time has stayed stopped for Leaf. It seems so cowardly to wait for the Will and then take it back to the Citadel . . . but what else can I do?*

The steam clouds ahead parted to show a long stone quay or platform that was only a few inches above the water level. Arthur dragged himself up onto it and collapsed. The Will watched from the water and began to flex the beginnings of its left wing.

Arthur hadn't lain there very long when he heard something other than the steady hum and clank of the steam engines. A more surreptitious noise — like someone sweeping the floor, accompanied by a faint patter of feet and the suggestion of a whistle . . .

He sat up and looked along the quay. The whistle was very quiet, but he thought he knew what it was, and his guess was confirmed as Dartbristle emerged out of the steaming mists. The Rat was holding a small crossbow in one hand and dragging a net full of something behind.

"Dartbristle!" Arthur called out.

The Raised Rat jumped, dropped the net, and lifted his crossbow with both hands.

"Lord Arthur! What are you doing here?"

"I got washed down a drain. But I'm glad to see you. I need some directions. What are you doing?"

Dartbristle was aiming the crossbow at him, while also shaking his head. Arthur saw with horrid fascination that the crossbow bolt had a head made of Immaterial Glass, like a sealed bottle, and a tiny piece of Nothing writhed inside.

"I'm sorry, Lord Arthur. I wish you weren't here! I have the strictest orders —"

"No!" shouted Arthur.

Dartbristle pulled the trigger, and the Nothing-poisoned bolt sped straight for Arthur's chest.

Chapter Eighteen

Arthur didn't have time to think or duck. He didn't need to. Without any active thought on his part, he leaned aside and caught the bolt as it passed, right in the middle of the shaft. The Nothing bottle on the end remained unbroken.

Arthur reversed the bolt to use it as a hand weapon and advanced upon Dartbristle, who was hastily cranking his crossbow to ready it for another bolt.

"The strictest orders," panted the Rat. "Shoot anyone who might interfere. I don't want to shoot you, but I must!"

Arthur stopped. Something — several somethings — were coming out of the steam clouds. Six Rat-catcher automatons, their long feelers testing the way ahead as they advanced down the quay.

Dartbristle saw the expression on Arthur's face and turned around, just as the closest Rat-catcher charged. The Rat threw his crossbow aside, picked up the net, and hurled it into the water. He tried to draw his long knife, but throwing the net had taken all the time he had. The

Rat-catcher's left claw caught him around the neck and snapped closed. Another automaton came up and wound its razor-edged feelers all around him and began to squeeze.

This was a mistake. Dartbristle was almost certainly already dead anyway, but the squeezing broke the Nothing bottles that were in their special wooden case on his back. Nothing exploded out, and the Rat-catchers' feelers instantly dissolved. The automatons hummed and squealed in alarm as the Nothing ran like quicksilver over their claws and out along their bodies, dissolving everything it touched.

In a few seconds, no trace remained of either Dartbristle or the two Rat-catcher automatons. The Nothing coalesced back into a puddle of darkness and began to sink into the bulwark bedrock, cutting a deep shaft through the reinforced House material.

Arthur eyed the remaining four automatons and readied himself for their attack. But they didn't charge. They waved their feelers around and their red central eye things glowed, and then the four of them turned around and disappeared back into the warm fog.

"Recognized you weren't a Rat," said the Will. It had two wings now, and was hopping along the surface of the pool, albeit without having any claws or a tail. "Which is lucky. I believe they have a bit of a problem with recognizing their legitimate prey."

"Poor Dartbristle," said Arthur. "He didn't want to shoot me, or at least not me in particular. What did he throw into the pool?"

"I shall take a look," said the Will. It scuttled across the surface and grabbed the floating net in its beak to drag it back to Arthur, who sat back down on the edge of the pool and let his feet dangle in the water. His boots had come off after all, in his rapid descent, and his coveralls were ripped to shreds below the knees and elbows. His belt was still on, fortunately, and Arthur tapped the pouch to confirm that the bag with the Key, the Mariner's medal, and Elephant was still there.

"These are things of sorcery," said the Will as it dropped the net near Arthur. "I do not know what they are for."

Arthur picked up the net. There were three large round glass floats inside. One red, one blue, and one green. They looked like the same kind of glass that Simultaneous Bottles were made from.

"He threw these into the water, even though it meant he didn't have time to draw his weapon," said Arthur. "It was that important."

"Then we should put them back in the water," said the Will. "To respect his dying wish."

"What?" asked Arthur. This wasn't the kind of behavior he was used to from any part of the Will.

"We should put them back in," the Will repeated. "As a matter of respect. Ah, the text for one of my tail feathers has just dropped in. Back in a moment."

It left Arthur holding the net and scudded off toward the waterfall that issued from the downpipe.

Arthur lifted the red float and looked at it. It didn't seem particularly sorcerous.

Arthur held the floats for a minute, thinking about something his mother had once said when she was explaining something to his sister Michaeli and didn't know he was listening. *There is never one absolutely right thing to do. All you can do is honor what you believe, accept the consequences of your own actions, and make the best out of whatever happens.*

"I bet I'm going to regret this," he said aloud, and dropped the floats back into the water. They bobbed around his feet and then slowly began to drift out, so slowly that he couldn't be sure if they were actually propelling themselves or if there was some kind of current.

Arthur watched the floats bob away and tried to plan what he was going to do next. But he still hurt all over — apart from the physical pain, he felt a great load of guilt.

I should've gotten Suzy to swim out with me. I wasn't thinking. I was too confident. No — I've got to stop obsessing. It's done now. I just have to rescue her. I'll have to challenge Saturday for the Key anyway. But she has too many sorcerers. So I should go back and get the Army. And Dame Primus, or Dame Quarto and Thingo or whoever. At least the other Keys. But if I do that, it might take too long. . . .

The Will came planing back on one claw a few minutes later, while Arthur wrestled with his conscience, his fears, and his half-formed plans.

"Almost there!" cawed the Will. "Only part of a claw and a tail feather to go!"

"Good," said Arthur. "As soon as you're ready, I guess we'd better go back to the Citadel —"

He stopped talking and cocked his head.

"What is it?" asked the Will. It was preening its wing feathers with its beak.

"The steam engines," said Arthur. "They sound closer."

He stood up and turned around.

"Closer and coming from a different direction."

The Will stopped preening and looked out across the water with its beady black eyes.

"Steamship," said Arthur. "Or steamships. That's what I can hear."

"I can see them!" said the Will. "Look! Eight of them."

Arthur stared out across the lake. There was too much steam and smoke, but even if he couldn't see anything, he could hear the rhythmic beat of the engines and the sound of the ship's wake. Finally one sharp bow thrust its way through the fog, and he saw the front of a Raised Rat steamship, with rank after rank of Newniths mustered on the foredeck.

"The Piper!" said Arthur. "We've got to get out of here!"

"So much sorcery!" said the Will. "Saturday is bound to respond at any moment!"

"I think she already has," said Arthur. He pointed up at the clouds of smoke above them. A huge ring of fire was beginning to form above the ships, a ring the size of an athletic track, easily five hundred yards in diameter. Flames began to fall from it, small flames at first, like fiery rain, but they began to get bigger and, from the way they changed color from yellow-red to blue and white, much hotter.

The ships responded by increasing their speed. They were heading straight for the quay where Arthur was standing, their funnels belching smoke as their engines were stoked for maximum power.

"They're going to run aground right here!" said Arthur. "Are you complete?"

"Not quite," said the Will calmly. "Just one short paragraph to go, but an essential one, to make a flight feather . . ."

"Hurry up," Arthur urged. As the ships came closer, the ring of fire was moving too, and the storm of incendiary rain was increasing in ferocity.

But it wasn't setting the ships alight, Arthur saw, or even hitting the Newnith soldiers on the decks. The rain was sliding off an invisible barrier that stretched from the masts of the ships down to the side rails, a sorcerous barrier that was, for the moment, proving impervious to Saturday's attack.

We don't have that barrier, Arthur realized. *That fire is getting way too close. . . .*

He could feel the heat of the flaming rain now, fierce on his face. The drops were so hot that he could see them keep going for several feet underwater, unquenched, their fire lasting for much longer than it should.

"Are you ready?" Arthur snapped again. "We have to run!"

"Almost, almost, almost there," crooned the raven.

Fiery raindrops were hissing into the water ten feet away. The ships, steaming at full speed, were three hundred yards away. A group of soldiers pointed at Arthur and suddenly there were arrows in the air, which flew true but didn't make it through the fire-storm.

"Done," said the raven. It flew up and perched on Arthur's shoulder. "I am complete. I am Part Six of the Will of the.—"

Arthur didn't wait to hear any more. He turned and ran along the quay as fast as he could go, flames spattering on the stone behind him. Steam klaxons sounded too, and the war cries of the Newniths, which he knew all too well from the battles in the Great Maze.

Through all that noise, through the hammering of engines, the scream of klaxons, the hiss and roar of the firestorm, and the shouts, there was still that other sound. A clear and separate sound, beautiful and terrible to hear.

The sound of the Piper, playing a tune upon his pipes.

"Ah," said the raven. "The Architect's troublesome third son."

"Troublesome!" Arthur snorted. "He's a lot worse than that."

The quay ended at a solid rock face, with no obvious exits. Arthur stared at it for a second, then started to hunt for protuberances or bits of stone that looked out of place. He quickly found one, pressed it, and rushed in as the rock-slab door groaned open.

The cavern beyond was an equipment room, the walls covered with racks of many different metalworking tools, which at a different time would have interested Arthur. With the Piper's Army landing behind him, he barely spared them a glance.

"How do I lock the door?" he asked the Will, after he made sure there was another exit.

"I have no idea," the Will replied.

"You've been here for the last ten thousand years! Haven't you learned anything?"

"My viewpoint has been rather limited," the raven explained. "Not to mention extremely fragmented."

Arthur grabbed several long iron bars and propped them up against the door, kicking them down so they were wedged in place.

"That might last a few minutes," he said. "Come on!"

"Where are we going?" asked the Will.

"Out of here, for a start." Arthur opened the far door and looked up a circular stairway made of red wrought iron that was decorated with gilded rosettes in its railings and on the steps. "The Piper will take a while to land all his troops, but they'll send out scouting parties for sure, and I guess Saturday will send forces down. We have to stay out of the way of both."

"Saturday may well be occupied high above," said

the Will. "Her tower has reached the underside of the Incomparable Gardens, and the Drasil trees are no longer growing taller."

Arthur started running up the steps, taking three at a time. The raven flew behind him, occasionally alighting on his head.

"Why does she want to get into the Incomparable Gardens?" Arthur asked as he climbed.

"Because the Incomparable Gardens are the first place the Architect made, and so shall be the last to fall," cawed the raven. "But also because Saturday believes that she should have always ruled there. She envies Sunday and would supplant him."

"Even if it means destroying the House?" asked Arthur. The stairway was winding up between walkways like the one where he and Suzy had arrived out of the Simultaneous Nebuchadnezzar.

It would be really easy to enter the Improbable Stair right now, he thought. *Going up these steps makes it really easy to visualize. . . .*

"She believes the Incomparable Gardens would survive even if the rest of the House crumbles into Nothing," said the raven. "She may even be correct. Making the lower parts of the House fall was the only way she could stop the Drasils from growing."

"So she'll get in? Can't Lord Sunday stop her?"

"I know nothing of Sunday's current capabilities," said the Will. "Nor his intentions. We must find and free Part Seven to help us with that. But first, of course, you must claim the Sixth Key from Saturday, the self-proclaimed Superior Sorcerer."

"I know," said Arthur. "But how am I supposed to do that?"

"Where there's a Will there's a —"

"Shut up!" protested Arthur. "I'm sick of hearing that."

"Oh?" asked the Will. "Heard it before? I do apologize."

"How about something a bit more concrete?" asked Arthur. "Like a plan, or some intelligent advice for a change?"

"Hmm," said the raven. "I take it my lesser Parts have not endeared themselves to you?"

"Not exactly," said Arthur. "Some bits are better than others. How long is this stair going to go up?"

"I do have a plan, actually," said the Will, after another fifty steps.

"Okay, what is it?" Arthur wasn't even slightly out of breath, despite running up so many steps. He still found that incredible.

"Your friend, the Piper's child, you want to attempt a rescue?"

"Yes," said Arthur.

If Suzy's still alive . . .

He stopped and the raven almost crashed into his face before managing to land on his shoulder. "Are you sure you're part of the Will?" Arthur had to ask. "The rest of you doesn't usually care much about . . . anyone, really."

"It's all part of my plan," the Will assured him. "You see, when I was suspended in the rain, I did get to visit many nooks and crannies that were rarely visited by anyone else. Including the hanging cages where they put prisoners."

"Hanging cages?" Arthur didn't like the sound of that.

"Yes," said the raven eagerly. "Now, on the south and west sides of the tower, there's all the big lifting apparatus and so on. On the north side it's completely sheer and undisturbed, I don't know why. But on the east side, there are lots of small extensions, platforms, balconies, crane-jigs, and such-like. Toward the top, around 61620, the Internal Auditors have a buttress that sticks out about fifty feet, and from that buttress they hang cages for prisoners. That's probably where your friend is now. Unless the Artful

Loungers killed her straight off. They are vicious creatures, and those Nothing-poison daggers of theirs —"

"Let's assume she's alive," Arthur interrupted. Then he hesitated before adding, "I want to rescue her — but how would we get to these cages and not attract the attention of the Internal Auditors? There's going to be a battle going on — maybe two battles. . . ."

"That will help us," said the Will. "But as to how we get there, it's rather simple. We disguise ourselves as a Bathroom Attendant."

"Ourselves?" asked Arthur. "As a single Bathroom Attendant?"

"Yes," croaked the raven happily. "You're almost tall enough to be a short Bathroom Attendant, and I can make myself into the mask."

"But why would a Bathroom Attendant go up there in the first place?"

Arthur shuddered as he remembered the gold-masked faces of the Bathroom Attendants who had washed him between the ears, temporarily removing his memory.

"Because they're Internal Auditors," explained the Will. "I mean, all Bathroom Attendants are Internal Auditors, though not all Internal Auditors are Bathroom Attendants."

"You mean they work for Saturday? *She's* the one who wants all the Piper's children's memories erased?"

"Yes, yes," said the Will. "It's all got to do with trying to delay the appearance of the Rightful Heir. Or, if you get knocked off, another one, and so on."

"So we disguise ourselves as a Bathroom Attendant, get to the Internal Auditors' offices, and rescue Suzy from the hanging cage. But how does that fit in with getting the Key from Saturday? Or anything else, for that matter?"

"Well, there shouldn't be any Internal Auditors there," said the Will. "They're Saturday's best troops, so they'll be up top, ready to fight their way into the Incomparable Gardens. Like I said, it's the east side, so it'll be the quiet side. We rescue your friend, then we watch the Piper's troops fight Saturday's troops and, at the right moment, you open an elevator shaft to the Citadel and bring your troops through."

"I don't know how to open an elevator shaft," said Arthur.

"It's easy — or at least it will be then, because all of Saturday's sorcerers that are stopping the elevators will be distracted. Or if they're not, you use the Fifth Key to take us out, we regroup, and then come back the same way. How does that sound?"

"Dodgy," Arthur said. "But the disguise part might work. If I can just rescue Suzy, and all three of us can get out, that's enough for now. I have to go back to Earth too. There's something important I need to —"

"Forget Earth!" insisted the raven. "Earth will be all right. It's the House we have to worry about."

"Isn't that the same thing?" asked Arthur. "I mean if the House goes, everything goes."

"Nope," said the raven. "Who told you that?"

"But . . . everyone . . ." stuttered Arthur. "The Architect made the House and the Secondary Realms. . . ."

"That's Denizens for you," said the raven. "She made most of the House after she made the Universe. I bet Saturday made up that 'Secondary Realms' stuff, the sly minx. The Architect made the House to observe and record what was happening out in the Universe because it was so interesting. Not the other way around."

"Most of the House," said Arthur intently. "You said 'most of the House.'"

"Yes, well, the Incomparable Gardens were first out of the Void."

"So they are the epicenter of the Universe? What happens if the Incomparable Gardens are destroyed?"

"Everything goes, end of creation, the jig's up."

"So basically what everyone has been saying is true," said Arthur. "It just means that until the last bit — the first bit — of the House is destroyed then the rest of the Universe will survive."

"I suppose so," said the raven. "If you want to get technical. Is that a door?"

It flew ahead, up through the middle of the spiral stair.

Arthur followed more slowly, deep in thought.

Chapter Nineteen

"Wait! Don't open it!" Arthur said, but it was too late. The raven had jumped on the handle and ridden it down, and then pushed the door open with its beak. On hearing Arthur's call, it turned around and looked back at him, with the door left ajar.

"Yes?"

Arthur reached the doorway and carefully looked through, out on to a paved square at the foot of the tower. There were two Sorcerous Supernumeraries only three or four feet away, fortunately standing with their backs to the door. Beyond them, the square was packed with a crowd of Denizens. There had to be at least two thousand of them, including hundreds of Sorcerous Supernumeraries and many more full sorcerers of varying ranks, all with their umbrellas folded despite the rain.

The Denizens had their backs to Arthur. They were all looking at a huge iron platform at the base of the tower. As broad and long as a football field, it was about twelve feet high. Made from thousands of plates riveted together, it looked like the deck of a very old battleship, with its hull and upper works sliced off.

Located next to the tower, the massive platform had a dozen twelve-foot-high bronze wheels along two sides. On each corner there were raised, open-roofed turrets packed with sorcerers.

But it wasn't the platform all the Denizens in the square were looking at. They were staring up at the construction that stood *on* the platform, which looked like a giant bullet. It was a cylinder several hundred feet high, with its bottom half solid bronze and its top half an open framework of bronze rods like a baroque birdcage. This caged section was divided into eight levels, which had woven wicker floors like in a balloon basket. The floors were connected by spindly metal ladders that ran up the full length of the cylinder, from the solid "cartridge" part to the top of the open section.

A dozen of the octopoidal construction automatons perched on the top of the rocket or whatever it was, flexing their tentacles. In the air around them flew fifty or sixty grease monkeys, their wings fluttering. Most of them held shiny pieces of metal.

Like the watching Denizens, all the grease monkeys were looking up. Arthur couldn't help but look up too, though he also eased the door shut a bit, to make it harder for him to be seen.

Blinking aside a raindrop that fell into his eye, Arthur saw a shape so dark, it had to be composed of Nothing. It was slowly descending out of the rain toward the bronze-wire cylinder, so slowly that at first it appeared to be levitating of its own accord. It was only after Arthur's eyes adjusted to its darkness that he saw faint lines of light upon its surface, traces made by the Immaterial ropes that were being used by several hundred flying Denizens to bring the object over to the bronze rocket.

The ropes were bright, but it was the dark shape that hurt Arthur's eyes. He immediately knew what it was: a spike of sorcerously fixed Nothing, like the one that the Piper had used to stop the movement of the Great Maze. This one was much, much taller, though it was also more slender. Arthur figured it to be a hundred feet long, with an incredibly thin, sharp point at the top.

The flying Denizens lined the spike up with the cylinder of bronze wire. When this was done, there was a shouted order from one of their number, and together they released the ropes. The spike fell straight down the remaining few feet and was caught by the automatons, whose tentacles were cased in some kind of protective coating that sparked and glowed as they handled the Nothing. They moved the spike around, shifting it to the right position, and lowered it into place. Immediately the grease monkeys moved in, fitting a collar of a sparkling translucent material — probably Immaterial Glass — to hold the spike in place atop the cylinder.

"Saturday's vehicle to pierce the underside of the Incomparable Gardens," said the Will, not quietly enough for Arthur's liking. He eased the door shut and turned on the raven.

"You need to be quieter and more careful," he whispered. "There are thousands of Denizens out there."

"I thought I was being quiet," said the Will, lowering its voice only a little. "I haven't been this corporeal for ages. It's hard getting used to having a throat . . . and a beak."

"Well, try harder to be quiet," Arthur admonished.

"Very well," croaked the raven, its voice so quiet that Arthur could barely understand it. "All I wanted to say was that if that's Saturday's vehicle for piercing the Gardens, then it's likely that all the Denizens down here will get in it. And when they get in it, we can get going."

"It must be the assault ram mentioned in Alyse's orders. And that's the Exterior Lift One or whatever it was called."

"It doesn't matter what it's called," said the Will. "As long as it goes. The sooner Saturday starts fighting with Sunday, the better for us to sneak up the other side of the tower."

"Okay." Arthur looked down at his ragged coveralls and bare feet. "I have to get some clothes."

"No problem!" said the Will. Before Arthur could stop it, it hopped to the door, pried it open, and hopped out, transforming as it did so into a small, extremely disheveled grease monkey.

He heard the Will say something to the closest Denizen, who answered loud enough for not only Arthur to hear, but every other Denizen within twenty yards.

"You sure? Asked for me, by name? Woxroth?"

"Yes," said the Will. "That was it. Woxroth. Just go in there."

Arthur pressed his back to the wall and wished that he'd set some firmer ground rules with the Will. He didn't even have his wrench, and he was wondering whether he could actually strangle the Denizen or just hit him with his fist when the Sorcerous Supernumerary came in, closely followed by the Will, who shut the door behind them.

The Supernumerary looked at Arthur, who raised both his hands, then his fist. When the Denizen just kept staring at him with a sad expression, Arthur lowered them again and said, "I just want your coat, hat, and boots. Hand them over."

"What?" asked the Denizen. "Haven't you got a letter for me?"

"No," said Arthur. He could feel the frustrated anger rising inside him again, the temper that appeared when his will was thwarted by insignificant creatures. "I am Arthur! Give me —"

There was a loud *thock,* and the Denizen suddenly crumpled to the ground. The raven jumped off the back of his head and dropped the cobble it had just used to great effect.

"What were you talking to him for?" it asked. "Should have just bopped him one."

"I was going to," protested Arthur as he bent down to take off the unconscious Denizen's coat. "He just looked so sad and pathetic."

The coat and boots adjusted themselves as Arthur put them on, but they weren't a bad fit to start with. Arthur looked down at himself and wondered if he'd grown even taller, possibly just in the last few minutes, because he needed to look like a Denizen. If the Will thought that he could pass for a Bathroom Attendant, he must be now almost six feet tall. Almost as tall as his basketball star older brother, Eric, he realized, a stab of melancholy passing through him.

Eric might already be dead; he'll die when the hospital is bombed and the city goes with it. I shouldn't be this tall, not for years yet. I feel like my old self is slipping away . . . faster and faster . . . and I can never be normal again.

He'd just finished dressing, had transferred his precious bag to his coat pocket, and was picking up the black umbrella when the door suddenly flung open. The Will, quick as a flash, transformed into a blanket and threw itself over the unconscious Denizen on the floor.

A sorcerer with a yellow umbrella looked in.

"Hurry up, idiot!" she shouted at Arthur. "We're boarding the assault ram! Come on!"

She stood there, watching as Arthur pulled the brim of his hat lower to hide his face and eyes, and tried to think. When he didn't move, she scowled and gestured with her umbrella.

"We haven't got all day! I'll put you on report in a minute. Woxroth, isn't it?"

"Sorry," mumbled Arthur. He started over to her, thinking that he might drag the Denizen inside and shut the door, and the Will could konk her with its cobble.

But there were more sorcerers looking in from behind her, their attention drawn by her shouting. So instead he just stumbled out the door. As he shut it behind him, he caught a flash of movement, and shuddered as he felt the Will run up his sleeve in the shape of something like a cockroach.

The waiting Denizens were no longer an unruly crowd, staring up at the bronze rocket. They were lining up in a long queue that zigzagged back and forth through the square. The head of the line was at the assault ram, and the Denizens there were climbing the external ladders on the solid bronze part and forming up in ranks on the different floors.

Arthur joined the line, the last in the long queue. The Denizen in front of him, another Sorcerous Supernumerary, looked back at him for a moment, but only gave a mournful sigh and trudged on. Arthur copied her pose, dragging his feet and keeping his chin tucked almost to his chest so his hat shielded his face.

It took quite a while to get to the rocket. Arthur had time to estimate the number of sorcerers climbing into the assault ram. By the time they all got on, he reckoned, there would be five thousand sorcerers on board. Most of them were full sorcerers too, some of them with umbrellas of gold and silver, which meant they were from higher levels he hadn't even seen. And right at the top, where they might have been all along, there were dozens of Denizens wearing the shiny satin top hats of Internal Auditors, the same as the ones the Piper had killed in Friday's eyrie in the Middle House. A contingent of Artful Loungers, in one of the middle levels, sat at the side of the rocket and kicked their legs through the bars.

As they approached the base of the ram, Arthur saw that there was a rainbow umbrella sorcerer checking everyone off a list. But even worse than that, there was also a very haughty-looking seven-foot-tall Denizen dressed in an immaculate silver tailcoat, night-black breeches, and super-reflective boots. He had a dove-gray greatcoat of seven capes draped over his shoulders, and any raindrops that got within a few feet of this sizzled themselves out of existence.

It's got to be Saturday's Dusk, thought Arthur. *He'll spot me for sure . . . and then there's five thousand sorcerers here to finish me off.*

Trying to act casual, Arthur raised his hand to his face and scratched his nose. With his mouth partially covered, he hissed, "Will!"

An albino cockroach with *Will* written on its back in red letters crawled up Arthur's wrist and into the palm of his hand.

Think to me, said the Will, silently. *You don't need to talk.*

Oh, yeah, replied Arthur. *I forgot. That's Saturday's Dusk up ahead. I think I need you to distract him. Take the shape of a Raised Rat, maybe, and run away. Then you'd better go rescue Suzy, because I'm not going to get the chance —*

You don't know that, the Will replied. *Also, I don't think Saturday's Dusk will know you. There's too much sorcery around for him to sniff you out. That bronze thing there is reeking with it, not to mention the platform it's on. They've got two hundred and fifty executive-level sorcerers preparing to lift that thing, you know. Just keep your head down.*

I still want you to go and rescue Suzy! Arthur insisted. *Go now, while there's still a chance.*

No, said the Will into Arthur's head. *My job is to find the Rightful Heir, and now that I have, I'm sticking with you. We might even get a chance at the Key. Anything can happen now, with the Piper's Army below and Sunday's insects above.*

I want you to go and rescue Suzy! I order you to do so!

"Name?" asked the gold-umbrella sorcerer.

Arthur dropped his hand, and the Will ran up his sleeve.

"Uh, Woxroth," muttered Arthur.

"Last and least," said the sorcerer. "Get up the ladder and find your place."

As Arthur scrambled up the ladder, the sorcerer turned to Saturday's Dusk, who had fastened a monocle in his right eye and was staring at the paved floor.

"Loading almost complete, sir."

"Not a moment too soon," replied Dusk. "The Piper's forces have finished landing and are moving up. Well, they may have the Floor. They will not get far up the tower, and we will soon be in the Gardens."

"Are they as beautiful and wondrous as they say?" asked the sorcerer as he started to climb, with Noon coming up after him. He was about fifteen feet behind Arthur, and the boy could hear every word.

"We will soon see," said Dusk. "Time we began, I think."

He held on to the ladder with one hand and cupped the other around his mouth, calling out to another gold-umbrella sorcerer who stood watching in the nearest corner cupola on the platform.

"Take her up!" shouted Dusk. "All the way to the top!"

Chapter Twenty

The Sorcerous Supernumeraries were on the lowest level of the rocket, immediately above the solid brass case. In between the holes in the wicker floor, Arthur could see the metal. He didn't want to think about what might be packed inside the lower half of the rocket. Some kind of propellant, he assumed. It was clear that the assault ram was going to be fired at the underside of the Incomparable Gardens, and the most likely place for that to happen was from the top of the tower.

Arthur was lucky to be one of the last aboard, because that meant his position was right up against the bars. The Denizens were packed in shoulder to shoulder, but he could turn around and see outside.

There was no talk among the sorcerers around Arthur. He looked out through the bars at the sorcerers in one of the corner cupolas on the platform below him. They were slotting their gold and silver umbrellas into holes in the ironwork. When the umbrellas were set, they turned the handles sideways to make them into something like music stands, and all together they placed open books upon the handles and, without any visible or audible signal, began to write with peacock-feather pens.

Arthur felt power in whatever they were writing. It made him feel slightly ill and itchy all over. As they wrote, the platform silently rose off the floor and began to climb up the side of the tower.

As it climbed, the Sorcerous Supernumeraries began to whisper to one another.

"We're all going to die."

"I bet I die first."

"We'll all die together."

"We might not. We might just be horribly injured and demoted again."

"You always look on the bright side, Athelbert."

"No, I don't. I do expect to get killed."

"Surprised they put us down here. Thought we'd be first to the slaughter."

"Nah, waste of time putting us up front. Those big beetle-things'd cut the likes of us up in a trice."

"What beetle-things?"

"Quiet!" roared an authoritative voice from somewhere farther inside the packed Denizen ranks.

Arthur shivered as he felt a new surge of sorcery from the writing Denizens in the cupolas, and the platform rose faster. He was on the far side of the rocket from the tower, so he couldn't see exactly how far they'd already risen, but looking down, he guessed they'd already gone up about two or three hundred levels.

"How come you've gotten a bit shorter, Woxroth?" asked a Denizen behind Arthur's back.

"Extra demotion," grunted Arthur.

Awed silence greeted this answer, followed by a muttered, "And I thought I had it bad. Demoted and then killed by a beetle, all in one day."

Optimistic lot, aren't they? said the Will into Arthur's mind.

They might be realistic, thought Arthur. *Do you have any suggestions about what I can do?*

Bide your time and look for any opportunity. Then take it.

That's really helpful.

"Sorcerers with a clear view to the exterior, stand ready!" ordered a voice from inside, the command echoed on the floors above.

The Denizens on either side of Arthur shuffled and pushed to get their folded umbrellas pointing out through the bars. Arthur copied them, though he didn't know why they were doing it.

"We're approaching 61600, top-out's at 61850. Be

prepared for a counterattack. If it's green and iridescent, shoot it!"

"Woxroth," whispered the Denizen to Arthur's left. "For the radiant eradication of matter, do we start by visualizing a glowing ember or the tip of the flame of a candle? I can't recall exactly. . . ."

"Uh, dunno," Arthur mumbled. He was trying to make his voice low and miserable, like the real Woxroth.

"An ember, of course," said the Sorcerous Supernumerary to Arthur's right. "Did you fail everything?"

"Almost everything," replied the left-hand Supernumerary. "Hoo! What's that? Glowing ember, glowing ember . . ."

"Hold on," said the right-hand Denizen. "They're our lot. On this side, anyway."

Arthur stared out through the bars. The platform was lifting the rocket up at a faster rate than he'd thought, at least as fast as the moving chain he'd ridden. So it was hard to see, with the air rushing through the bars, the slight rocking motion of the rocket, and the constant mild jostling of all the Denizens.

Several hundred feet above them, and closing rapidly, the sky was crisscrossed with smoky trails and sudden, sparking lights that blossomed like silent fireworks in brilliant colors, lasting only a few seconds. All Arthur could hear was the breathing of the Denizens around him, and the low hum of the moving platform.

The sparks were being fired up and out by thousands of flying Denizens who formed a circular perimeter several hundred yards out from the tower, surrounding it. At first Arthur couldn't make out what they were casting their silent, sparking spells at, there was so much smoke and light in the sky. Then he saw a green tendril that had to be at least four hundred feet long and ten feet thick suddenly lash out of the cloud and strike a flier who had dared to climb too high. The tendril cracked like a whip, and Arthur and all the Denizens flinched at the sudden noise and the sight of the tendril smashing the Denizen's wings. The lash must have terribly injured the sorcerer as well, for he or she fell like a lump, straight down.

"Lashed to bits by a weed, that'd be right," said one of Arthur's neighbors.

"Nah," said someone else. "That's a good fifteen hundred feet up. They're going to fire this thing from the top, a bit short of weed range, and we'll slice through those tendrils like a hot knife through a butter cake. 'Course, after that, we'll be easy pickings for the beetles."

"I've never even seen a butter cake."

Arthur only half-listened to the complaints behind and

around him. He watched the tendril strike again, still flinching at the whip crack even though he knew it was coming. But the Denizen who'd said they wouldn't get close was right. The platform had slowed down a lot and was now maneuvering sideways. Arthur could feel less sorcerous energy being expended by the Denizens in the driving cupolas.

The platform was also rotating, Arthur saw as his view changed. The corner of the tower came into sight and then the entire side. They were level with the top now, the ground out of sight at least seventeen thousand feet below.

Here at its peak, the tower was much, much narrower than the levels Arthur had visited. The last fifteen levels were the narrowest, composed of only five offices a side. At the very top, right in the middle, there was a single, much larger office that was the size of four of the usual cubes. Though its frame was iron, it had clear crystal walls and a roof made of the same material.

Someone was inside this crystal office, watching the platform and the rocket slowly slide across toward . . . toward *her*, Arthur saw.

Superior Saturday. It had to be her. She looked eight feet tall at least, and Arthur couldn't tell if she had shining blond hair or was wearing a metallic helmet. She was certainly wearing some kind of armor, a breastplate of red-gold that shone like the setting sun, and leg and arm armor made from plates in different shades of evening sunlight.

The platform was turning so that the door in the lowest level of the rocket was lined up with her office. The door that Arthur was standing next to. The door that Superior Saturday clearly intended to use. . . .

"Make way! Let's have a path through!" called the commanding voice. Denizens pushed at Arthur, driving him away from the door, packing him in even tighter against his comrades as a path was cleared from the doorway through to the interior ladder that led up to the next level of the rocket.

A Denizen pushed back right into Arthur's face, but he didn't complain. He shifted a little to his right and peered through the two-inch gap between two Sorcerers' shoulders in front of him.

Superior Saturday touched the wall of her office and the crystal fell away, shattering into motes of light that spun around and wove themselves into a pair of shining wings that fell upon her shoulders and flapped twice as she launched herself across the empty air to the aperture between the bronze bars that served as a door for the rocket. She landed as if she were dancing in a ballet, and strode through the crowd without a sideways glance at the Denizens who bent their heads and tried to bow, despite the cramped space and many painful cranial collisions.

There, in her hand! called the Will. *The Key. You could call to it. No, on second thought, best not yet —*

Definitely not, thought Arthur. He stood on tiptoe and craned his neck to see what it was that Saturday held in her hand. It wasn't an umbrella, or even anything as large as a knife, just something slim and short. . . .

It's a pen, thought Arthur. *A quill pen.*

He lost sight of it, and Saturday as well, as she climbed up the interior ladder. The platform rose up some twenty or thirty feet and drifted across to line up with the middle of the tower. Then, with a flourish of peacock-quill pens, the entire platform settled on top of the tower with the groan and shriek of iron upon iron. A minute later, dozens of automatons climbed up and grease monkeys flew up from below and started to fix the platform to the tower.

Arthur looked across and up. It was hard to estimate, but he thought the clouds were only eight or nine hundred feet above them, and the tendrils that were still snapping down could reach about three hundred feet. So they had a six-hundred-foot safety margin. Presumably the assault ram had to be this close in order to have a chance of breaking through the underside of the Incomparable Gardens.

Someone shouted far below. Arthur looked back down. The grease monkeys and the automatons were disappearing back under the platform.

"Brace for launch!" called out the commanding voice inside the rocket.

The Denizens around Arthur grabbed the bars, and the Denizens farther in grabbed one another. Arthur took a firm grip on the closest bar and bent his knees.

"Light the blue touchpaper!" called out the voice.

Arthur couldn't see exactly what happened then, but somewhere over in the middle of the rocket, there was a sudden eruption, a vertical jet of white-hot sparks that reached the wicker floor above but somehow did not set it alight.

"Five . . . four . . . three . . . two . . . one!" called the voice. "Fire!"

There was a loud fizzling noise, and nothing happened.

"Fire?" repeated the voice, somewhat less commandingly.

"What is going on down there?" asked a clear, cold female voice that made Arthur shiver. "Must I do everything myself?"

"No, milady," called the first voice, which was now

beseeching. "There is a second touchpaper. I will light it myself."

A minute later, there was another violent stream of sparks.

"Five . . . four . . . three . . . two . . . one . . . um . . ."

A violent force struck the rocket, sending every Denizen to his or her knees. Arthur was thrown from side to side, smacking into the sorcerers around him, their umbrella handles smashing into his ribs and thighs.

Huge clouds of smoke billowed up and out, and the rocket stormed up from the platform, accelerating faster than anything Arthur had ever experienced before.

Four seconds later, he heard the terrible crack of a tendril from above, closely followed by several more.

Crack! Crack! Crack!

The rocket shook with each impact, and the bronze cage rods rang like bells. The assault ram did not deviate from its course, straight up into the underbelly of the Incomparable Gardens.

"Brace! Brace for impact!"

The warning was too late for most of the Denizens. Very few were still on their feet, the floor around Arthur resembling a particularly crazy game of Twister.

When the assault ram struck, everyone hit the ceiling and bounced back down. Arthur was bashed by what he thought was every possible combination of elbows, knees, umbrella points, and handles, and if he were still human he knew he would have broken every bone in his body and probably had several stab wounds as well.

But he was not human, which was just as well, for a human mind would have had as hard a time as a human body. As the rocket sliced through the underside of the Incomparable Gardens, the interior became suddenly dark. Then, as some of the less-addled Denizens began to make their umbrellas glow with colored light, they saw rich dark earth spewing through the bars, earth that flowed in like water, threatening to drown and choke them.

"Ward the sides!" someone shouted. Umbrellas flicked open, and Denizens began to speak spells, using words that lanced through Arthur's forehead, though it wasn't exactly pain that he felt.

The opened umbrellas and the spells stemmed the tide of earth. The rocket began to slow, and the anxious Denizens below heard cheering and shouting above. Then the rocket stopped completely, with nothing but the rich earth to see around them.

"Top floor's through!" called out a Denizen from above. "We've breached the bed!"

"Come on!" shouted someone else. "To the ladders and victory!"

Arthur scrambled to his feet, umbrella in hand. He was barely upright before he was knocked down again by a Denizen who screamed as she fell, her hands desperately gripping a huge, toothy-mawed earthworm that had struck through the bars. The earthworm was at least part-Nithling, for its open mouth did not show a fleshy throat, but the darkness of Nothing.

Arthur stabbed the worm with the point of his umbrella.

Die! he thought furiously and at the same time. *Glowing ember . . . candle flame . . . whatever, just die!*

Chapter Twenty-one

A six-foot-long flame of blazing, white-hot intensity struck the worm and ran along its length without touching the Denizen it was trying to eat. She continued to hold its ashy remains for a millisecond, then, as they blew apart in her hands, she clapped and said, "Cor!"

"So *you* didn't fail advanced blasting," said someone else. "Still, something let you down, made you just like us . . . ow! Another one!"

Flames, shooting sparks, and bolts of frost shot out of numerous umbrellas as more of the huge, toothy earthworms thrust through the bars. Denizens shouted and screamed and fought, many falling to Nothing-infested earthworm bites and strangulation, as well as one another's sorcery.

"Up! Up!" someone roared. "We have to get clear! This is not the battle!"

"Could have fooled me," grunted someone close by Arthur's ear, as he blasted another striking worm back into the earth it came from.

"Up!"

Arthur obeyed the command, backing towards the interior ladder. The Denizens behind him and the Sorcerous Supernumeraries at his side had the luxury of turning around, but the worms kept coming in. A shrinking ring of Denizens and constant sorcerous attacks were all that kept them back.

Finally, there was only Arthur and four other Denizens around the base of the ladder, desperately flaming the boiling sea of worms that was writhing and arching towards them.

"We can't climb up — as soon as one goes, they'll get the rest of us!" said a Denizen. "I knew it would end like this —"

"Shut up!" yelled Arthur. There were too many worms, and his lances of flame could only kill a few at once.

There's so much sorcery happening here, he thought. *No one could possibly notice me add some more.*

Arthur reached into his coat pocket with his left hand while he batted at a worm with his umbrella, temporarily just a lump of metal and fabric. One-handed, he fumbled open the bag that held the Fifth Key, pushing two fingers in until he touched the cold, smooth glass of the mirror.

"By the power of the Fifth Key," he whispered, so low that he could not even hear himself above the hideous frying sounds of burning worms, "destroy all the worms about me. Make them as if they had never been!"

There was an intense flash of light, accompanied by a single pure note of the most beautiful music, and the worms were gone. Even the ash and the burned bits of worm-meat were gone as well, as if they had never existed.

"Right," said Arthur. He could hear shouting, explosions, and the hissing sound of fire and destruction spells going on up above. "Up!"

The other Denizens looked at him, then turned and climbed at a speed that would have won them approval from Alyse.

"They are more afraid of you than they are of the worms," chuckled the Will. It flew out of Arthur's sleeve as a three-inch-long raven, and grew to full size as it landed on his shoulder. "I should wait a moment before going up. She knows you are here now."

"What?" asked Arthur. "But I thought, there is so much sorcery . . ."

"Not of the kind made possible by the Keys," said the Will. "But it is a good time. She is beset by Sunday's defenders. We will assail her when they have done their work. Best to wait here 'til then."

"Here?" asked Arthur. As if in answer to his question, the whole rocket shuddered and the floor suddenly dropped several feet and lurched to one side.

"Maybe not," conceded the raven. "Quick! Up!"

Arthur went up the ladder and the next and the one after that so fast, he almost felt like he was himself a rocket. But he had to slow down as he caught up to the line of Denizens. They were climbing quickly too, for the rocket was shaking and shifting. Looking back down, where the floors were still illuminated by the fading light from the umbrellas of dead Denizens, Arthur saw that parts of the assault ram had fallen away . . . or had been torn off.

"Hurry up!" shouted the Denizen ahead of Arthur. "The ram's falling apart!"

She looked down and hastily amended, "I mean it's falling back down!"

Arthur looked. The lower floors of the rocket were no longer there. Instead there was a gaping, roughly rocket-sized hole, and at the end of it there were wisps of cloud. A long way below that, he could see a fuzzy green lump that was the top of the tower.

"Hurry up!" screamed the Denizen again, and everyone did hurry up, as more and more bits of the rocket fell away below them and went down through the hole to either strike the tower or perhaps make the even longer journey — all twenty-odd thousand feet to the floor of the Upper House.

Arthur burst out on the top floor of the ram like a bubble from the bottom of the bath. The Nothing spike was gone, consumed by its purpose in cutting a way through the bed of the Incomparable Gardens.

Except it hadn't quite cut all the way through, or rather the rocket hadn't. Arthur looked around quickly, blinking at the soft, mellow sunlight. The top of the ram was about twenty feet below the rim of the hole made by the spike. Some of the interior ladders from the rocket had been ripped off and propped against the earth. From the shouting and general tumult, Arthur figured that's where everyone had gone.

The floor fell under Arthur's feet, slipping down several yards. He ran for a ladder and jumped halfway up it. As the floor fell, Arthur sprinted up the rungs, taking four at a time. Three rungs from the top, he hurled himself up with all the energy and concentration of an Olympic high-jumper. The Will helped too, gripping his head and flapping with all its might.

Arthur just made it, landing on the rim of the hole with his legs dangling, his fingers clawing into soft green turf that threatened to give way. Then he was scrabbling forward to safety, as the top floor of the assault ram and a dozen luckless Denizens fell away behind him.

Before Arthur could get his bearings, he was almost cut in two by a pair of giant elongated jaws. Desperately he rolled aside, thrusting his umbrella up at the twelve-foot-long iridescent green beetle that loomed over him.

The beetle grabbed the umbrella and crushed it to bits, which would have been a good tactic against a normal sorcerer. With Arthur, it just gave him time to get the Fifth Key out of the bag. He held it up, focused his mind upon it, and the beetle inverted to become a mirror image of itself. Then it dwindled like a receding star into a mere pinprick of light.

There were many more beetles, but none were close enough to do harm. Arthur took a few seconds to take stock.

He was standing on a wonderful green lawn of perfect, real turf. It was in the shape of an oval, at least a mile wide, and was surrounded by a low ridge of heather and wildflowers, surmounted by a fringe of majestic red and gold autumnal trees that blocked further sight.

Only a hundred yards away, there was a ring of large silver croquet hoops, and it was here that Saturday and her remaining forces were defending themselves against a tide of long-jawed beetles. A long line of mainly headless Denizen bodies led from the hole behind Arthur to the ring of hoops. There was quite a pile of bodies near Arthur, so he ran over and crouched down behind this makeshift wall. None of the beetles came after him.

"You're all right," said a voice by Arthur's knee. He recoiled in horror as a Denizen head without a body scowled up at him. "Typical. Everyone else always has the luck, with promotions and everything. We'd better win, is all I can say. Are we winning?"

"I don't know," said Arthur. It was difficult to tell what was happening. There were still at least a thousand sorcerers, plus Saturday herself. They'd made a kind of shield-ring of open umbrellas, and from behind that they were shooting spells of fire and destruction, explosion and implosion, unraveling and transformation. But there were at least as many of the beetles, and they were ripping sorcerers out of the shield wall and pulling them apart with their long pincer jaws.

"She's winning this round," said the Will. "She's using the Key on them, as well as ordinary sorcery. Look."

Saturday loomed tall in the middle of her troops, with two almost-as-tall Denizens at her side. She held the Sixth Key almost casually, like an orchestra conductor might hold her baton. As Arthur watched, she carefully wrote something in the air. A line of cursive, glowing letters twined out of the pen to make a flowing ribbon in the air.

When Saturday finished writing and flicked the pen, the ribbon of words flew over the heads of her sorcerers and bored straight through first one beetle, then another and another and another, as if it were a thread flowing behind the needle of a quick-handed seamstress. Wherever it passed, whether through head or limb or carapace, the beetle fell to the ground and did not move again.

"I think now is the opportunity," said the Will. "Claim the Key. It will come to you when you call."

"But she's still got a ton of sorcerers, and those beetles are dropping like . . . like flies," said Arthur.

"I know, but what else is there to do?" asked the Will. "I told you I'm not so good with plans. Besides, she's going to notice us in a second."

"Think. I have to think," muttered Arthur. He looked around. Where could he go if he got the Key? The trees were too far away, and probably housed more horrible insects. He had no idea what lay beyond them. He had no idea if Lord Sunday would intervene, and if he did, on whose side.

Saturday's use of the Sixth Key had already been decisive, in only a matter of seconds. At least half of Sunday's beetles lay dead or at least immobile around the ring of defensive umbrellas. More were falling, to the cheers of Saturday's sorcerers.

"She's noticed us," said the Will. "Sorry about that. I think I moved my wings too much."

Saturday was staring straight at Arthur, and so were her two cohorts, her Noon and Dusk.

Arthur looked behind him and made a decision. Transferring the Fifth Key to his left hand in one swift motion, he held up his right hand and called out as loudly as he could.

"I, Arthur, anointed Heir to the Kingdom, claim the Sixth Key —"

Lightning flashed from Saturday's hand. It forked to her Noon and Dusk, and then forked again to the sorcerers around them, splitting again at the next lot of sorcerers. Within a second, it had a hundred branches, and then in another second, a thousand, the force of Saturday's spell multiplying exponentially. As all the branches left the last line of outer sorcerers, they combined back to form a lightning strike greater than any ever produced by a natural storm.

The bolt came straight at Arthur. He raised the mirror, thinking to divert or reflect it, but it was too strong. He was blasted off his feet and thrown back twenty . . . thirty feet . . . the Will cawing and shrieking at his side.

Arthur hit the dirt on the very edge of the hole. For a second he teetered there, on the brink. His hat fell off the back of his head, and the Will grabbed his arm so hard that golden blood welled up under the bird's claws as its wings thrashed the air.

"And with it the Mastery of the Upper House," shrieked Arthur as he finally lost his balance. "I claim it by blood and bone and contest . . ."

He fell, but even as he fell, he called out, his words echoing up to Saturday and her sorcerers.

"Out of truth, in testament, and against all trouble!"

Chapter Twenty-two

Leaf had only managed to move twenty people when Martine came back. The older woman did not offer any explanation, or even talk. She just appeared as Leaf was grimly trying to lift one of the sleepers onto a bed, and took over. Leaf gratefully assumed the role of lifting legs as Martine heaved the sleepers up under the arms.

In an hour, they moved fifty people to the operating theater complex and Leaf began to hope that there was a chance they would move them all. It was a small hope, but it was better than the drear fatalism that earlier had sat like a cold weight in her chest.

They were moving the fifty-first, fifty-second, and fifty-third sleeper when the clock started to turn over again.

"Oh, no!" Martine cried as she saw the display slowly — very slowly — transform from 11:58 to 11:59.

"It's still slower," said Leaf. "Time. It's moving slower. We have more than a minute. Maybe it'll be really slow, we can go back up —"

Martine pushed the bed with sudden energy, pushing harder than she had before, too fast for safety, sending it rocketing out into the corridor so that it collided none too gently with the far wall. She pushed Leaf too, as the girl hesitated, thinking that maybe, just maybe she could get back up and get a few more sleepers, save just a few . . .

The clock turned to 12:00.

Leaf and Martine ran for the bed.

"Arthur, you have to come back and stop this now!" Leaf shouted at the ceiling. "You can't let this happen!"

Martine grabbed the bed and turned it towards the operating theater. Leaf sobbed and bit back a cry and started to push.

They were halfway along the corridor when the ground shook and all the lights went out. The shaking continued for at least a minute, and there was a terrible rattle and bang of things falling, some of them foam ceiling insulation tiles that fell on Leaf.

Then the ground was still again. Leaf crouched in the darkness, by the bed, holding Martine's hand. She could not think of what she should do, her mind paralyzed by what had happened.

"I can't believe they did it," she said. "And Arthur didn't come back. And we only saved . . . we only saved so few . . . I mean to be saved from Friday, only to get killed without even waking up . . ."

"We don't know what's happened," said Martine, her voice scratchy and unfamiliar. "We'll have to find out."

Leaf laughed, an hysterical giggle of fear and anxiety that she only just managed to get under control. As she stifled it, the green emergency lights slowly flickered on, illuminating Martine's face as she bent down to look at Leaf.

"I'm sorry I ran away," said Martine. "You're braver than I am, you know."

"Am I?" asked Leaf. She choked back a sob that was threatening to come out. "You came back."

"Yes," said Martine. "I think Arthur will come back too."

"He'd better!" snapped Leaf. She stood up and checked the three sleepers. They were fine, apart from having a fine coating of dust and a few fragments of broken insulation.

"You hear that, Arthur!" Leaf said, looking up at the exposed wiring above her head. "You need to come back and fix everything up! You . . . need to come back!"

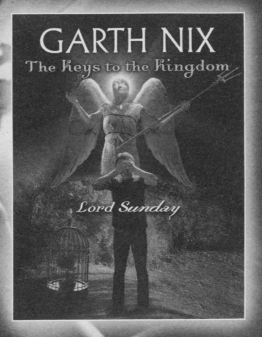